David Lloyd

The Legend of Captain Jones

Relating his adventure to sea, his first landing, and strange combat with a

mighty bear - Vol. 1

David Lloyd

The Legend of Captain Jones
Relating his adventure to sea, his first landing, and strange combat with a mighty bear - Vol. 1

ISBN/EAN: 9783337090876

Printed in Europe, USA, Canada, Australia, Japan

Cover: Foto ©Andreas Hilbeck / pixelio.de

More available books at **www.hansebooks.com**

Fames windy trump blew up this haughty mind
 To do or wish, to do what here you find :
Twas ne're held error yet in errant Knights
(which priviledge he claims) to dress their fights
In high hyperbolies : for youths example,
To make their minds, as they grow men, grow ample.
Thus such atchievements are assaid and done
As pass the common power and sence of man.
Then let high spirits strive to imitate,
Not what he did, but what he doth relate.

THE
LEGEND
OF
Captain *JONES*:

The First and Second Part.

Relating his Adventure to
Sea : His first landing, and strange
Combat with a mighty Bear. His furious
Battel with his six and thirty men against the Army
of eleven Kings, with their overthrow and deaths. His relieving
of *Kemper* Castle. His strange and admirable Sea-fight with
six huge Gallies of *Spain*, and nine thousand Souldiers. His
being taken Prisoner, and hard Usage. His being set at Liberty
by the Kings command, and return for *England*. Also, his
other incredible Adventures and Atchievements by Sea and Land ;
continued to his Death.

LONDON,

Printed for *Francis Haley*, and are to be fold at his
Shop at the upper end of *Chancery lane*, next
Holborn, 1671.

To the READER.

Eader, y'have here the Mirrour of the times,
Old Jones wrapt in his colours, and my rimes.
ceive him fairly (pray) nor censure how,
what he tells : the matter hee'l avow.
d for the form he speks in, I'le maintain it,
comes as neer his vain as I could strain it.
r 'twere improper to set forth an Asse
pparison'd, and pannel a great Horse.
'y part claims no inventions praise : for (know it)
here ere there's fiction in't, there he's the Poet.
is last deeds here epitomiz'd, intreat
me thundring pen to set them forth compleat.
t him whose lofty Muse will deigne to do it,
rink Sack and Gunpowder, and so fall to it.

A 3

Οἶον ἔπινε μόνον, κ' αὐτὸς καὶ ὁμήλυδες ἄνδρες.
Αὖτε θερμαίνουσα πόσις τὸ πρόσωπον ἔφλεξε·
Ὡς φάτο, καὶ Μίνως ὁ δικασπόλος ἀντίον ηὔδα,
Τίφθ' ἀφαμαρτοεπὲς φλυαρεῖς Ἀσκληπιε; οὐδὲν
Οὔτ' οἰνοφλυγίας ὁράᾳς σημεῖον, ἢ ὅρα
Πινομένα τελετῆς, Φοιβηὰ οὐδὲ καὶ ἄθρει,
Αἰεὶ σωφροσύνης Ἥρως ἐᾷ μεμηλε καὶ ἀϊδῶς,
Θαυμάσια γὰρ ῥέζων καὶ ὑπερβαίνοντα πενιχρὰν
Ἀνδρομέων πίστιν ψυχῶν ἐφοβεῖτο κε μήπως
Ψευδόμενος φαίνοιτο, τὰ δ' αἴτιόν ἐστιν ἐρευθὺς
Τῦτο ἀκουόντεσσιν ἀρέσκετο γνώμη ἀνακτος
Ἐλυσίοις πεδίοισι γέλως κ' ἄσβεστος ἐνῶντο.

fter Captain *Jones* his great Conqueſt in the
Indies, theſe Verſes were ingraven on a Pillar
of Gold, in the famous City of *Chiapa.*

H Avacun! at ſiquinta, rucar, ruchaquit, a l olem,
Rut ſi nut ſiquin Jonos, *quintacque* Britanno ;
rutisba Dios, *chiru narapata tiquita,*
alocohta naloc quinquimi, naxa tinuloc,
aquil Ruchaquil, Don Spanos, *Cacaracart a*
ra Ixnulocoſh Europon *quincel amoloh,*
inaloconta nucam quiti Chicata Chiapa,
ecoacana mani quinraphi tilcona rutat,
rurapa cochor vilcat Cacunta, Chalocoh
avocohta ruvac, Rixim car nucar avixim ;
locon-hita quimac, avix inreca corochi,
n Nut ſi nuchac, quinrochi nutisba China ;
ipam Rumoloh mac, numac taxa veronquil
yrvo capat quiro vinac navecata maniquir,
ilocontho Navos *uutacqui Coave-caca,*
yirvani vilquin Xinvi nucamca tivito.

D

By

*By the assistance of Mr. Gage his rules to learn tha
Indian Tongue call'd* Poconchi, *thus faithfull
and verbatim translated into English.*

HO Paſſenger ! Behold, read, underſtand,
Great *Jones*, a Britain, conquer'd all this Land ;
In thirteen dayes twelve Kings he overthrew,
And millions of Salvages he ſlew :
At laſt the *Spaniſh Dons* with all their force
Of *Indian* foot, and *Europæan* Horſe,
Surpriz'd him near *Chiapa*, where he ſtood
Five hours in fight cover'd with fire and blood ;
And in that furious conflict, all his men,
Who were once thirty ſix, reduc'd to ten.
With thoſe few blades, and his own mighty Arm,
He did repulſe them without ſpell or charm :
Then to his Ship retreated ; and to ſhew
'Twas Glory, and not Gold, he did purſue,
Of all the ſpoils he took but one rich Cup,
And as much Gold as made this Pillar up.

This Monument ſtood Undefac'd 1588. *But Imme
diately after was demoliſht by the Envy of th
Spaniards, and the Gold converted to other uſes.*

E. LI

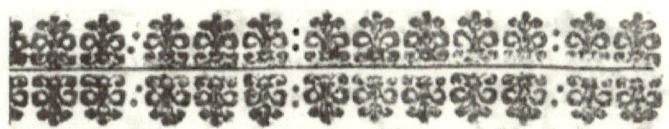

On the REVIVAL of
Captain JONES.

WHy shak'st thou Coward Hand? dost drop the Pen,
    Honour'd to limne the Prodigie of Men?
That means this strange Surprizal that unknits
Thy joynts, possessing them with Palzy Fits?
Who dares (dread Heroe) offer to thy Fame,
(Without Apollo's Call) must feel the same.
Mov'd by pure zeal to Honour, thus I run
A young Enthusiast the Priests among,
Trembling to pay my Mite. Welcome once more
To us, Great Britains Mars; our joys run ore
To see the truth of a Platonick year
Confirm'd in thee; so bright dost thou appear
Deckt with thy valours Rayes: Poets (who can
Make Gods) have rais'd thee up, thou God-like Man,
What brave Revenge had'st th'ad on thy old Foe,
Hadst thou but breath'd our Air some moneths agoe?
Thou, and thy six and thirty set on shore
In Hispaniola, would'st have acted more
Than was (I blushing write it) done by ——————
And —————— with their ten thousand men.

I acquiesce, and leave to higher Forms
Thy stern deportment in all Fights and storms;
Who draw at large, and well ; my single Hint
Is a Portentous Act in a small Print.
Reward those who again have made thee breathe,
With Laurel ta'ne from thy victorious wreathe ;
I have enough t'entitle me to Fame,
Who both a Britain am, and of thy Name.

H. I.

ar selves: I see his marble frown,

ning afhes challenge their renown,

hus. Durft your narration

ble acts of admiration,

rm'd, when *Æolus* deny'd

e 'gainft the ftrugling tide?

tial man affronted worfe,

b'd him to retard my courfe.

e fend to *Lapland* for a wind,

n'd, I had enough behind;

oftern, I fent forth a blaft

ils, and crack'd the fturdy Maft,

riggot with fuch force, that it

e, and fo was like to fplit.

cy, this I forefaw,

ances I had help at Maw;

an up of Englifh Beer,

ng water) I made ufe of here;

nduit pipe ore deck, and Spouted,

hoar, fo that Saint *Patrick* fhouted,

friends, this is no time for mirth,

luge comes to drown the earth!

Obstructions being removed in this sort,
At length I landed in an Irish port,
And thought it wisdom, before they came to treat,
To stay my stomack with a bit of meat.
Seeing a Cook hang up a stall-fed Ox,
I bad him roast it quickly, with a pox;
'Twas quickly done : as soon as off the Spit
My Valiant grinders snapt it at a bit,
Sooner than one could turn his hand about,
As when a Pickrel swallows up a Trout.
The Cook's amazed : what, quoth I, thou thief,
I do not eat, but barrel up my beef;
I can lay up a whole one and a half,
The Ox that *Milo* carried was a Calf :
Sirrah, make haste, get me some more meat drest
To fortifie the Castle of my brest.
I mean to feed, as Dromedaries do,
Both for the present, and the future too.
Thus terrify'd, my foes ran to the bogs,
And there were Metamorphos'd into frogs;
I speedily destroy'd that croaking faction,
Then could no longer live for want of action.
Death, natures beadle, took me by the hand,
And said, Grand Captain, I thee now disband:
Abstract of valour, let thy name be blest,
Lie down within this tomb, and take thy rest.

On Valiant *Jones*.

Come see the Man, whom *Mountains* bred,
who talked high, as he was fed.
No Court like Milk-sop train'd tot'h fiddle,
But yeand i'th' Region call'd the middle.
There *Captain Jones* his cradle chooses,
More dangerous then that of *Moses*;
for that was watch'd by *Pharaos* daughter,
The *Deabe*, a Nurse, did him look after,
Or he for them: Come Wolfe, or goat
who took the Nibb, and fill'd his throat;
thence was ally'd to *Brute*; neer Cuz
by th' nurses side to *Romulus*:
And for his nimbleness and skipping,
Remus (himself) could nere out leap him;
This, and the marbles of his throat,
came from the *Rennet* of the goat
curdling his gutturalls: His haire's
all flaggy too, and rank as theirs.
Which was resented, as was *Mars*,
Or *Hercules*, for his black A----
These were strange signs, and did betoken
what ere was after by him spoken.

B 4

'Twas

'Twas well the wars were done before
Lost in Llewellin *and* Glendore.
Had Jones *liv'd then, in vain th'* Assails
Of Saxons; *wales had still been wales.*

    Nay had the fates (but they deny'd,
For Jones *had neither barn nor Bride)*
Sav'd but his Præpuce in Skincks *fight,*
That spoyl'd his skirmishes by night.
No doubt an Issue, not of's legs,
But of his Loyns, for he lov'd eggs
Extreamly to the very bowels,
would have out-Vavasord the Powels:
Content us therefore with those duels,
which no man did, or very few els,
Related from his mouth : This Brit,
As Cæsar did, could he have writ,
what Comments had he made ? what storys
Of Irish wolves, which now are Torys?
This Frontispiece alas ! nay, twenty,
As big as this, had been too scanty;
The Elephant and's Pego-man,
And Hob's on his Leviathan,
Nay, what so ere old Inigo
(His namesake) could have drawn for show
Had been too small a Scene: why then
No more, it shrivels up my Pen.

On the Legend of Captain Jones.

Reader, be ſtout and credulous, for he
    Muſt have both Courage and credulity
That reads this Poem ; and to have enough,
His ſoul ſhould be half Cheverel and half buff :
For *Jones* ſuch things doth talk, and ſuch things do
As far tranſcend all Faith and Reaſon too.

   Thoſe ancient Poets that, in former times,
Extol'd their *Heroes* with undying Rhimes,
Muſt go to ſchool to learn of *Jones*, for he
At once both made and writ all Chivalrie.
There *Homer* and *Achilles* both muſt club
To make one ſtory, this muſt fight, that dub.
Which asks Time, Charge, & Danger; whilſt bold *Jones*
Does without either, raiſe, and kill at once,
Tam Marti quam Mercurio, if he liſt,
He could diſpute, as well as fight with fiſt.
With one Cuff-ſyllogiſm confute more men
Then Wit or Reaſon could convince with ten.

   'Mongſt all the Giants whom he robb'd of breath,
He has three ſignal Battels fought with Death,
While Fame, that ſtill hates living men, gave out,
That *Jones* was conquer'd ; and to clear the doubt,
Employ'd the Wits with a lamenting pen
In Epitaphs to kill him o're agen.

   At which enrag'd he roſe, and ſwore *they lye* ;
  Jones is not dead ; I ſwear *Jones* ſhall not dye.

A. B.

Upon Captain Jones *Relating his own Exploits.*

Loe here great Captain *Jones*! in whom do dwell
Both *Mars* and *Mercury*, gods stout and fell;
Thou, thine own Trump, dost with a valiant voice
Both beat thy Foes, and thy great Conquests noise;
Thus thy *Minerva* lends thee speech and shield,
Wherewith thou all things mak'st unto thee yield;
Ajax, Ulysses, both in thee agree,
Thy valour and thy tongue alike are free;
Great *Alexander's* Envy would have ceast,
Nor would *Achilles* fate have spoyl'd his rest,
Had but *Jones* Poetry inspir'd his Soul,
To whom, the blind man *Homer's* but a fool;
Homer cou'd only his borrow'd phancy write,
Jones cou'd do more, both strangely feign and fight;
Cæsar, of all the Worthy's, most like Thee,
He did both fight and tell's own History,
Which yet compar'd with thy Relation
Seems but an old thred-bare narration;
So between both how vast's the Difference,
Jones doth all *Cæsars* baffle, and all Sence.

I. V. Oxon.

On the same.

AWay with Fictions; short of our stout man,
The Poet must now turn Historian;
His fights, his fights, his fights, his victories,
His conquests, his trophyes, and yet no lyes !
What Wars were they when all each battel fell
But Jones, and he surviv'd, his services to tell?
When he relates the story, an Enemy
Truth fears to be, lest in contending, she
Too late learn due subjection; thus the tyde
Forces the waters that would gently slide :
When our great Jones had quite subdu'd the land,
He boldly puts to Sea; but here's a stand,
The Sea of such an adversary proud
To try'm, its waves into a storm doth crowd.
Jones leaves his ship, he scorned such a flood,
For he had often swam in streams of blood;
He then such Tempests rais'd with arms and back,
That th' very Ocean did fear a wrack.
Yet he would dye, that th' shades might of him fear,
And learn, by Mortals woe, great Jones to fear.

N. H.

Upon the incomparably valiant, Captain *JONES*.

WHen I do read thy Legend, *Jones*, and see
    Thy Fights, thy Victories, thy All, and Thee,
I stand engag'd 'twixt Wonder and Delight,
That I can neither think, nor speak, nor write.
My Faith thou puzzl'st, and Invention too,
'Tis monstrous strange! but these things thou didst do;
Alcides, Hector, are out-done by Thee,
Thy History hath foil'd all Poetry.
Poor *Hector*! he by his own Valour's lost,
But thou surviv'st, and dost thy Triumphs boast.
Herc'les, we know, hath his *Non ultra* found,
But to Thee, *Jones*, nor Earth, nor Sea's a bound;
The World, from East to West, from North to South,
To eccho forth thy Fame's but one wide Mouth.
The Earth, Great *Jones*, grows fruitful in thy praise,
And all her car's to crown thy head with Bayes.
The Sea payes Homage to thee, and roars out
Brave *Jones*'s name, who's greater far than *Cnute*.
Neptune to Thee his Trident doth resign,
The Whales cry out, with trembling, We are thine;
And proud of thy Command, they swell the Main,

For

r thy great fake thronging into a Train;
ien *Spain* does yield to thy fierce heat; thy might
oftrates their doughty *Don*, *Diego* hight;
iy arms fo tofs'd that vap'ring Admiral,
if ha'd nought been but a Tennis-ball.
iou didft Bears, Lyons, and fuch Monfters quell;
' thy ftrong hand the fturdy El'phant fell.
e the bright Sun peep'd from his Eaftern bed,
even Kings before thy feet, brave Jones, lay dead.
hat work wouldft thou have made in one whole
idft thou but found for thy *Killzadog* play? (day,
iw fuch exploits, fo ftrange, thou couldft atchieve,
ine ever yet coud tell Brave Jones, and live.
or Mortals we! the Fates have thought it fit
efhould in wonder fpend our dayes and wit.

P. D. Ox

?🌸🌸🌸🌸🌸🌸🌸🌸🌸🌸🌸🌸🌸🌸?

Have you not heard of Jones, that man of wonder,
That brough Don Dego & Mac-kil-Cow under?
And when he had um there, agreed, being wise,
To run away before that they should rise?
For 'tis a Maxime; If youl'd be secure,
Still make the Reliques of a Conquest sure:
Jones still kill'd those that fled, and only those;
For such tuff Fellows as withstood his blows
He scorn'd and spar'd; thinking it base to beat
A stubborn Enemy that won't retreat.
  'Mongst all those blustering firs that I have read
(Whose greatest wonder is that they are dead)
There's not any Knights, nor bold Atchievers Name,
So much as Jones's in the Book of Fame:
They much of Greeces Alexander brag,
Hee'd put ten Alexanders in a Bag:
Eleven fierce Kings, backt with two thousand Louts,
Jones with a Ragged Troop beats all to Clouts.
But sure it was a Conquest by Compact,
For he could never be aecus'd of Fact:
And yet no story a Romaneer sings,
That ere exploited more stupendious things;
Quixot a winged Gyant once did kill:
That's but a flying tale, believ't who will:
This were but petty hardship, Jones was one
Would skin a Flint, and eat it when h'had done.
  Had Jones but been alive, and seen the pudder

Betwixt

'etwixt Briganza's *Legate* and Anstrudder;
hen the fierce Portugal in high Bravado,
Storming th' Exchange with Pistols and Granado)
'ut the poor *Pego-mongers* to a *Rout,*
And their beloved Bables flung about:
Hee'd not have fawn'd upon um like a Spaniel,
ones would have kickt the Dog into the Kennel;
And spight of Darkness made his head ring Noon,
'or daring to pluck Honour from the Moon:
H'had dyed no other Death, for furious Jones,
Once flesh'd, would kill ten such, and make no bones:
  He once had an encounter with a Lyon.
Though most believe he never durst come nigh one)
'ut as the Author says, and I believe,
Both bravely fought, and many wounds did give
Each other, till the Beast in woful dumps
Worn out, (for Jones *had fought him to his stumps*)
n honour of his Fall and Jones's *Glory,*
Di'd with meer Age, and there's an end oth' story.
  Many a tough adventure he hath had,
And like a true Knight Errand, ne're a bad:
He foil'd great Asdriasdust *in the twink-*
ing of an eye, as easie as to drink:
And yet as tough, and dry a sir, as ere was yokt
Into a sword (Jones *often wisht him chokt)*
But yet, of all the Gyants that came nigh him,
There's Nerapenny *stuck the longest by him*;
'or *though his slender wounds made many doubt him,*
That thread-bare Tear-coats he had still about him;
And if they say he had not, he's belyed,

For he had ne'r a peny when he dy'd.
   Jones had a valiant stomack, and would eat
As well as fight, provided he had meat,
Else patience upon force took place, for Jones
Kept many fasting dayes, and made no bones.
But I'de not have you think it was for want ;
For when he had no Money, nor Provant,
The Fowl flew to his Table, and the Fish
Left the cold stream, and swam into his dish.
'Tis an old Proverb, (Like to like, they say)
Jones was a Cods-head too as well as they.
   But Jones, like a Disease, both Sexes smites ;
For he wounds Ladies too as well as Knights :
He was so trim a youth, the Queen of No-land
Thought him some Princely Shaver come from Poland ;
And so he prov'd indeed, for by Guds duds
He most unkindly left her in the Suds ;
Jones like a wiseacres begg'd to be spar'd,
For he had No-land, nor for No-land car'd :
If any ask you wherein lay his Grace ?
Venus lov'd Mars his Truncheon, not his face.
   To wind up all, Fame's Trump his Deeds doth tell,
   Although a sow-gelders would do't as well.

W. T.

THE
LEGEND
OF
Captain JONES.

I Sing thy Armes (*Bellona*) and the Mans
  Whose mighty deeds out-did
  great *Tamberlans* :
  Thy Trump (dire goddess) send,   *The Invo-*
    that I may thunder   *cation.*
Some wondrous strain, to speak this man of wonder.
  When Fates decreed that *Captain Jones* should be
The life and death of men, they could not see
A place more suiting to bring forth this mirror
Of Martial spirits, this thunder-crack of terror,
Then some vast mountains womb, whose   *His birth-*
  rigid rocks   *place.*
Might form him, and foreshew the hardy knocks
              C   Which

Which he fhould give and take : Nor were they nice
To think it bafe, that mountains bring forth mice,
Since from a Brittifh mount and *Mars* his ftones,
They fent this Man of men, ftern *Captain Jones.*
Wild Mares milk nurft him on the mountains gorfe,
Which gave him ftrength and ftomach like a horfe ;
Goats flefh matur'd him, kill'd on craggy tops,
Which taught him to mount Rampiers like thofe rock
Ere eighteen winters fully waxen were,
This imp of *Mars* began to doe and dare.
With *Reymond,* a ftout brother of the fword,
He firft attempted Sea, and went aboard,
Two hundred ftrong, for the Eaft Indies bound,
Fame was the only prize he fought or found.
Twice twenty days aufpicious waves and winds
Lull'd them : then *Æolus* and *Neptune* joynes
To work *Great Jones* his fall.   Envy and ire,
To fee him more then Man, made them confpire ;
Rough *Boreas* whiftled to the dancing fhip,
The boifterous billows ftrove to over-skip
The bounding veffel. In this great difafter
Reymond, the fouldiers, Mariners and Mafter   *His ftou*
Loft heart & heed to rule, then up ftarts *Jones,*   *behaviou*
Calls for fix Gifpins, drinks them off at once.   *in a ftor*
                                                      at fea.
Thus arm'd at all points, yet as light as feather,
He afcends, and drew, and pift againft the weather,
And are we born (my hearts, quoth he) to die?
Shall we defcend? Thy immortality
Neptune thou muft refign, if I come thither :
One Sea may not contain us both together.

Nor waves nor winds could fright him with the motion
Who thought he could contain and piſs an Ocean.
His fatall *Smiter* thrice aloft he ſhakes,
And frowns : the Sea, and Ship, and canvaſs quakes :
Then from the hatches he deſcends, and ſtept
into his Cabbin, drank again, and ſlept.
When theſe rough gods beheld him thus ſecure,
And arm'd againſt them like a man pot-ſure,
They ſtint vain ſtorms ; and ſo *Monſtrifera* *The name*
So hight the Ship) toucht about Florida,   *of his ſhip.*
Upon a deſart Iſland call'd *Crotona;*
Where ſavage beaſts and ſerpents live alone :
Here *Jones* would needs to land, though *Reymond* ſwore
Danger was in't: he laught, and leapt aſhore, *His land-*
Danger(quoth he)to thē who dangers fright, *ing.*
My heart was fram'd to dare, my hands to fight.
Some ſix and thirty more put forth to ground,
Theſe for freſh food, he for adventure bound ;
They limit their return when three hours ends,
Which *Reymond,* with the ſhip at Sea, attends.
Theſe Sea-ſick ſouldiers, range hills, woods, and vallies,
Seeking provant to fill their empty bellies ;
Jones goes alone, where fate prepar'd to meet him
With ſuch a prey as did unfriendly greet him ;
A Bear as black as darkneſs, and as fell *His en-*
As Tyger, vaſt as the black dog of hell, *counter*
Runs at him open jaw'd, ſo fierce, ſo faſt, *with a*
That he no leiſure had to draw for haſte *Beare.*
Kilzadog his good ſword, with fiſt he aim'd, *The namᵉ*
Ill arm'd, a blow, wᶜʰ ſure the bear had brain'd, *of his*
      But *ſword.*

But that between her yawning teeth it dings,
The gauntlet there ftuck faft, his hands he wrings
Unarm'd. unharm'd from thence ; her foremoft pawe
The Bear on *Jones* his fhoulder claps, and gnawes
The gauntlet wedg'd between her teeth: *Jones* clafpt he
With both his arms, and ftrove by force to caft her.
And here they try a pluck, and grafp, and tug,
And foame ; but *Jones* who knew the Cornifh hug,
Heaves her a foot from footing, fwings her round,
And with a fhort turn hurles her on the ground ;
Then came his good fword forth to act his part,
Which pierc't skin, ribs, and riffe, and rove her heart.
The head (his trophee) from the trunk he cuts,
And with it back unto the fhore he ftruts,
Where *Reymond* was appointed to attend
His and the refts return : but he (falfe friend)
When they were once on fhore and out of fight,
Hoift failes to fea, and took himfelf to flight.
Here *Jones* found fraud in man, and deeply fwears
Revenge on *Reymonds* head, the reft he chears ;
All fafe return'd, but all in defperation   *He joyne*
To fee themfelves left there to defolation :   *himfelf*
Nor grain nor ground, but wild ; nor man,   *the 36 f*
                    (nor beaft,   *diers.*
But favage ; yet (O ftrange) here *Jones* doth feaft
His fix and thirty daily, 'twas with fifhes   *His tak*
Toft from his halberts point into their difhes ; *of fifh*
Wherewith he took them ftanding on the fhore *with h*
Out of the Ocean : whether 'twas the ftore *halberts*
Frequenting this unpeopled coaft, or whether *point.*

To fee this wondrous man they fhould together
And fo aftonied, yield themfelves a prey
To him from whom they durft not fwim away,
Be't fo, or fo, I'le not decide, but I
Know *Jones* tells this for truth, who knows no lye.
Thus from his weapons point, nine moneths they fed,
Till fate Sir *Richard Greenfield* thither led,
Who to America tranfports with *Jones*
His fix and thirty fifh-fed Mermydons,
To Infip were they brought and left ; oh then
'Twas time, had they had meat, to play the men.
Their firft encounter there with famine was,
A dry and defart foile, nor grain nor grafs,
Nor drink, but water had they here, nor bread *Captaine*
For thrice twelve moneths, but caves for houfe *Jones*
(and bed. *encoun-*
ters with
Such living as that Country could afford *the great*
Bold *Iones* was forc't to win by dint of fword. *Giant Af-*
Eleven fierce Kings poffefs the fertile tract *driafduft.*
Of this great Coaft, who all their powers
(compact
To vanquifh *Iones* : a brave attempt 'tis true,
Yet more then twice eleven fierce Kings could doe.
Two thoufand choice and doughty men they chofe,
To bid him battle, arm'd with darts and bowes,
And arrowes fadome long, well barb'd with bone
Of fome ftrange fifh, which pierc't through fteel and
(ftone ;
And thus they come prepar'd : When they drew neer
(him,

C 3   H

He brought his soldiers forth, and thus did chear them
My five and twenty friends (for only those
Had fate & famine left) these darts and bows
Are fit to deal with fearful Crows and Daws,
But us whose hearts of oak and empty maws,
Hungers sharp dart hath pierc't, & yet we stad with the
To fright & foil our foes with sword in hand)
These weapons cānot conquer, nor the number
Were they two thousand such as *John aCumber*.
Doth hunger bite you ? bite your foes as fast,
Eat these men-eaters (souldiers) kill and tast.
Would you gain glory ? Kill by six and seaven,
If Crowns of Kings, then here behold eleven.
And this he spake and drew. With stomack fierce
They give the first assault; Now for a verse
To speak *great Jones* his deeds, who headlong goes
Amongst the thickest ranks, cuts, kills, & throws,
Some by the legs, some by the waste he makes
shorter : another by the lock he takes,
Reaps off his head, wherewith he brains another,
Then at one stroke kills father, son, and brother ;
Few scap'd with life, but strangely ; happy those
Which scap'd with loss of half a face or nose.
Nor may I pass his men, who cut and slash,
Like those that fought for life, not Crowns or Cash.
Want made them seem (which sure their foes dismaid)
The very sons of death, whose parts they plaid ;
The Insips now uo aime can take aright,
They think each foe they meet, a mighty Sprite ;
And so they fly. Six Kings he took, and kil'd,

His oration to his 25 souldiers before their fight with the 2000 sent against him by the 11 American Kings.

His courage in fight.

Five,

Five, with eight hundred soldiers left the field ; *5 Kings*
Twelve hundred fell: for those that went off safe *& 1200*
Their heels & not their hearts the praise he gave. *soldiers*
Unto their fullest towns, whē he had kild them, *slain.*
He brought his ragged regiment, and fill'd them.
Here on the river of Mengog they find
A Weare with fish of wondrous growth and kind,
Where with a thousand herrings they were fed, *Strange*
All two foot long besides the tail and head. *Herrings*

   Here some may ask what came of all the wealth,
For *Jones* brought nothing home besides himself)
This conquest gain'd; sure many precious things *What be-*
Must needs attend the death of six such Kings. *came of*
 answer briefly ; His heroick desire *the rich*
Ascends above earth excrements as fire : *prizes.*
Nor can descend to Crowns. The souldiers found
Much wealth, which in their home-return was drown'd;
till fortune favours *Jones.* Amidst this river
He spies a sail directly bearing thither ; .
He calls, and finds them English, homeward bound,
Who for fresh water thrust into the sound.
With these his men and he for England comes, *He & his*
Had England known it, all her guns & drums *men come*
Had been too little to express her joy, *for Eng-*
As when victorious *Hector* entred *Troy* ; *land.*
Yet ere he can attain his native coast,
Æneas-like he must be tyr'd and tost
With storms, till meat and water wax'd so scant.
that *Jones* drank nought but piss one week for want.

     C 4   At

At laſt when they had caſt out all their goods,
(To ſave themſelves) into the furious floods,
The ſhip all bruis'd with ſands, and ſtorms, and ſtones
At *Ipſwich* doth disburthen the ſea of *Jones.*
England ſalutes him with the general joys
Of Court and Country, Knights, Squires, fools, & boy
In every town rejoyce at his arrivall,
The townſmen where he comes their wives do ſwive all
And bid them think on *Jones* amidſt this glee,
In hope to get ſuch roaring boys as he :
Others this joy, into a fury rapt
To ſing his praiſe, though elegant and apt ;
Yet mixt with fictions, which he ſcorns. 'tis known
Jones fancies no additions but his own ;
Nor need we ſtir our brains for glorious ſtuffe
To paint his praiſe, himſelf hath done enough,
And hath preſcrib'd that I ſhould write no more
Then his good memory hath kept in ſtore
Of what he did. Perhaps he hath or can
Doe more, but hides it like a modeſt man.
His Britiſh expedition makes me hie.
From his vagary to his Chivalry.
This Dukedomes confines pointing on the South,
Great Keper Caſtle guards on Morligs mouth ; *His raiſing*
Which key of Britain (like great Britaines   *of the ſiege*
                       (Dover) *of Kempet*
                                Caſtle.
Was well nigh loſt by ſiege till *Jones* went over,
To dye or raiſe it : 'Twas begirt by land
With fifteen thouſand. Four tall ſhips withſtand
All ſuccours from the ſea : Againſt this force

                                          He

e goes as boldly as an eyeless horse,
With one small Bark (the Shit-fire 'twas) a hot one,
nd save a hundred men was with him not one :
ut these were Welsh blades, born for hacks & hewing,
nd car'd not what they did so they were doing.
Thus like some tempest these four ships he frightens,
His guns roare thunder whilst his powder lightens,
nd from his broad side poures a showre of hail ;
Which rakes them thorow & thorow, ribs, mast, & sail.
Their shot replies, but they were rankt too high
o touch the Pinnace, which bears up so nigh
nd playes so hot, that her opponents think
ome Devill is grand Captain of the Pink.
One English Pirat with them, whilst he watches
His time to shoot, spies *Jones* upon the hatches,
And cryes out, Ho, hoise Canvas all at once.
And fly, or yield ; Zounds it is *Captain Jones.*
The man swore reason, and 'twas quickly heard,
or, not a Bullet like that name was feard ;
They fly, he follows, but a partial wind
And wings of fear sav'd them, left him behind.
To Kemper he returns him, and supplies it
With fifty men, and victuals to suffice it
ix moneths : the foes by land lose hope and heart
To oppose this new supply, and so depart :
Then on the Gate this title was ingraved,
Jones rescued Kemper, and the Dukedome saved.
Thus plum'd with Laurell, *Jones* for England came,
Where George of Cumberland, rapt with his fame,

Wooes

Wooes him to be Vicegeneral of his fleet;
Which *Jones* vouchfaft, becaufe he was to meet
Men like himfelf, the doughty Dons of Spain
Whofe honour (or lofe all) he vow'd to gain.
And better fate in this defign he wifhr no',
The to cope fingle wth their great *Don Quixot.*
Stay Mufe and blufh, and figh & fing no more;
Here *Jones* his miftrefs, Fortune, plaid the whore.
Yet, whilft thou loath'ft her lightnefs to rehearfe,
Let indignation make thee chide in verfe;
Ah deity! and blindly to go on fo
From thy deare minion *Jones* to *John D'Alonfo,*
Whofe out and infide is no better mettle
Then an old Drum, or a bafe Tinkers Kettle.
And tak'ft thou him for *Jones*? that glorious boy,
Whom Venus felf would kifs (were Mars away)
Well, fickle goddefs, if thou be divine,
I'le fwear, heaven hath, like earth, light feminine.
Twas thus, This fleet cut through the Weftern main
And fo lay hovering on the coaft of Spaine:
Jones led the front (as 'twas his cuftom ftill)
The firft in fight, laft to be kil'd or kill:
His fhip went fwifteft too, as did his mind
On honours wings: But (oh) an envious wind
Fild all his fail, and wrapt him in a mift
From being feen, or feeing, ere he wift.
And thus he loft his train, and caft about,
And beat thefe Seas five days to find them out;
Till in his queft it was his fate to meet
Don Iohn **D.** *Alonfo* with the Spanifh fleet.

Th

s general bid amain, and *Iones* defi'd
m Canons mouth. The Don again repli'd
/ith four for one. Ah *Iones*, had I my wish,
ome Godhead should have turn'd thee to a fish,
o escape this dire assault ; thou shouldst not then
3e taken like a tame beast in thy den.
ie thousand souldiers was the force that fought
is day with *Iones*, whom six huge gallies brought,
e stoutest boats to make a bold Bravado
at were in Spains invisible Armado :
es first commands his men to take their victuall,
: souldier-like drank much, and pray'd a little ;
en tells them briefly, here's no place to fly,
me friends, let's bravely live or bravely die.
this the gallies had inclos'd him round,
d sought to board him ; but they quickly found
e ship too hot to grapple with so soon,
d so bore off again, and paid her room.
en each by turn present her the broad side,
hich she repaid with interest, and so ply'd,
at where her bullets pierce, whole streams of blood
 out through the gallyes ribs, and dye the flood ;
e foes disdain thus long to stand in fight
ainst one, and so press on with all their might :
d now the storm grew hot, and deep in blood,
Mad rage had got the place where reason stood :
ns, drums, and trumpets stop the souldiers ears,
om hearing cryes and groanes ; and fury reares
is fatall combate to so strange a height,
at higher powers express th'effects of fright.

Great

Great Neptune quakt and roar'd, clouds ran and pil
The winds fell down, and Titan lurkt in mist.
Then belch huge bullets forth, smoak, fire, & thund
Their fury strikes the gods with fear and wonder,
One gally which two hundred slaves did row,
Affront the ship, in hope to buldge her prow.
Jones gave her leave; but when she once came nig
Out bursts his murdering shot; here doom'd to dye
Down dropp'd the brave Viceroy of Saint Iago,
Don Diego de Cordona, and Gonzago.
Stones, chains, and bullets tare their passage out
Through men and galley; which soon tackt about
In hope to get aloose; but *Jones* sent after
Two lucky shots, which light twixt wind and water.
  " In crept the quaking billow, where he spide
  " Those holes, in hope its fearful head to hide;
  " The galley like afeard, or whose hurt, doth creep
  " Into the trembling bowels of the deep;
  " And so she sank. Thus Diego whilst he try'd
His force with *Jones*, with fifteen hundred dy'd.
Now *Jones* all breathless sat to take his breath
Upon a But of sack, and drank the death
Of *Don John de Alonso*, which his men
Pledge in a rowse, and so they fight agen.
Ninescore there were, but threescore now remain
To do or suffer, for the rest were slain.
The Spanish force distract twixt hope and fear,
Yet by their fellows fall forewarnd, forbear
This hot assault, keep distance, and at *Jones*
Let fly their shot at random all at once,

                                        So

ome half a Cable short, and some flew ore
he top saile, some the stern and rudder tore :
One, all the rest in fatall fury past,
and all to shivers rove the master mast,
Down fell the tackle, and the vessel lay
in English prison and a Spanish prey.
tarboard and Larboard side, from poope to prow
They all let drive, and rak'd her through and through.
All now but *Jones* and one man more were kill'd,
Who cry'd, *Now fight and die, or live and yield.*
Jones kill'd the first, the latter he besought him
Upon his knees, whilst by the knees he caught him
Begging for life, a bullet took away
His head, which when 'twas off still seem'd to pray ;
Out flew the head and bullet both at once
Between the manly thighes of Captain *Jones* :
Who lookt behind him, art thou gone (quoth he)
Still may they die so, that cry yield to me.
Now nought to him but blood and death appear'd,
Death was his wish, captivity he fear'd ;
Which to prevent Kil-za-dog forth he drew, *This*
And thus he spake, Brave Cato, Cato slew, *sword be*
And when victorious Brutus could not stand, *won from*
He fell, but by his own victorious hand. *the great*
Brutus, I am a Brute, and have thy spirit, *ful Gyant*
Thy fortune and self-death I will inherit. *Nereapeny.*
Thus said, his sword unto his side he plyes,
Which his good Genius stays & thus replyes ; *His genius*
  Hold *Jones*, reserved for thy Countrys good, *dehorts him*
Born to shed hostil, not thy home-bred blood, *murder.*

                                    And

And know that felf-death is the Cowards curfe :
For, he that dyes fo, dyes for fear of worfe ;
The time will come when Irifh bogs fhall quake
Under thy feet, whilft great Oneale doth fhake.
I may not on thy future deeds dilate,
Thy fword muft right what is involv'd in fate ;
This know, in thy old age thou fhalt impart
Unto thy Countries youth thy martiall art,
Teach them to manage arms, and how they muft
Make bright their fwords, which peace hath wrapt
     Now *Jones* vouchfaf'd to live, not for himfelf   (r
But for his Countries good, and common wealth ;
His fcarlet cap he dons, with crimfon plume,
And he afcends the hatches all in fume.
The Musketiers ambitioufly defire
To hit this mark, and all at once give fire :
Some Bullets raze his plume, his haire, his nofe,
His velvet Jerkin, and his fattin nofe ;
(The fcars may yet be feen) yet draws he breath
Fearlefs, and harmlefs, in the jaws of death.
    The Spaniard now conjeƈtur'd his intent,
By feeking death t'avoid imprifonment,
And fo forbore to fhoot, drew near and fought
To take the prey, which they fo dear had bought.
    Then *Jones* all raging throws into the main
That fword which men and wolves and bears had flain
That fword which erft had drunk the blood of Kings,
Into the bowels of the deep he dings.
The Ocean thirld for fear, and gave it place,
And greedy Neptune fnatcht it for his mace.
                                        *T*he

Then from the ship he leaps amongst his foes,
and so undaunted to *Don John* he goes,
Who bid him Live, *Don*-like, but gave him breath,
Onely to breathe in greater pains then death.
This shock had sent to Styx six thousand men,
Whose souls *Don John* to satisfie again   *How he*
inflicts more servile punishments on *Jones*,   *was used*
Then countervail six thousand deaths at once.   *being ta-*
                                                   ken captive
He beds on boards, is fed with bits and knocks
Ape-like, bare-foot with neither shooes nor socks.
Hair shirt, blew bonnet, made a servile knave,
A lowsie, dusty, nasty galley-slave.
At last he brings *Jones* to the Spanish King,
And sayes : Great Monarch, see this precious thing ;
six thousand of your bravest men he cost,   *He is pre-*
Who to gain him alive , their lives have lost;   *sented to*
Nor think the bargain dear, for here's a man   *the Spanish*
Can doe & say more then your Viceroy can.   *King.*
This praise was given him by the crafty *Don*,
for fear his loss seem'd more then what he won ;
and so it did indeed, for *Philip* thought
ones inside by his outside dearly bought.
To try he asks him, whither bound, and whence
He was, and *Jones* replies with little sence;
Whether through fear or faining, he affords
To all the King demands, not three wise words.
To try him further, in a Jaile they cast him,   *He is cast*
Which serv'd for nothing but to stink & fast   *in prison.*
and here it was his destiny to light   (in
pon a learned Priest, a Jesuite :

                                        With

With him falls *Iones* to work. The sacred word *He di*
His weapon was, for he had drown'd his sword. *ted the*
Their question was of purgatory, where,   *with a*
And whether 'tis at all, if so, 'tis here   *suit ab*
(Quoth *Iones*.) For he half tir'd with pains   *Purgat*
                                    (would needs
Go straight to heaven : And thus the question bree
Iones was no Schoolman, yet he bore a brain
Which nere forgot what ere it could contain.
Yet this old Priest so wrests the letters sence,
Equivocates, denies plain consequence,
Starts to and fro, and raiseth such confusions,
That *Iones* chief ward was to deny conclusions :
But, do this subtill Schoolman what he can,
Such was the vigour of this martiall man,
Though he was no good disputant or Text-man
Nor knew to spell *Amen*, to serve a Sexton ;
Yet truth, with confidence, and his strong fist
Doth first convince, and then convert the Priest.
Some talk of *Garnets* straw, and *Lipsius* lasses;
Whose miracles made many Artists asses ;
But here's a miracle transcends them all,
An Artist made wise by a Naturall.
   Now Englands Court rings all of *Iones* his *Order ta*
                                    (fetters, *ken inEn-*
                                              land for h
And men of rank were soon sent ore with let-*vansome.*
                                    (ters,
To ransome him for gold, or man for man,
On any terms. The King with many a Don
Consults upon this point : One thought it fit

                                              T

To deal upon exchange ; some better wit
Thought it more fit to keep this second Drake, *The point*
For so he term'd him wisely, and thus spake ; *of his ran-*
Armies are Englands arm, Captains the hand *some deba-*
Of this strong arm that rules by sea & land : *ted in Sp.*
And of this arm and hand I think in sum,
This captive Captain is the very thumb,
This speech was short and sound, but could not go so
Without th'opposing of old Don Mendozo ;
VVho lov'd and favour'd *Iones,* but knew not why,
(Nature it seems had wrought some sympathy)
  Pardon (quoth he) (dread Sovereign) are we come
To talk of arms and hands and Captain Thumb ?
From East to VVest our Arms and armies reign,
And fear we now for one to re-obtain
So many Viceroys in the Isle captiv'd,
For us, of light and almost life depriv'd ;
VVere Drake's and Candish spirit in this dragon,
Let not their future times have this to brag on,
That Englands Queen did prize one Captain more
Than Spains great Monarch did his twenty four.

His speech prevail'd, and so they all attone,
And twenty four were askt and given for one ;
All which had led great armies to the field,
And never knew but once, what twas to yield.
And thus was *Iones* dismist ; yet ere he go
The King, to grace him, made him kiss his toe.
Long maist thou live old man, and may thy tongue
And memory, as thou grow'st old, wax young :

D   Then

Then wilt thou live in fpight of time, and be
Times fubject, and time thine t'imblazon thee.
  Pardon my forward Mufe, ftriving to foare
A pitch with thee at mid-day tyr'd, gives ore ;
For, who can fpeak thee all (thou mighty man ?)
Not Greece's *Homer*, nor Rome's *Mantuan*.
Thy Irifh warrs, thy taking great *Tyrone*,   *A touch o*
Whole heards of Wolves kill'd there by thee *fome othe*
                              deeds of
                    (alone, *chivalry by*
Thy feveral fingle duels with fierce men   *him per-*
And bears,all flain;and that dry journey wher*formed.*
Thou drankft but what thou pift for thrice feven days.
Which made thee dry ere fince,then th' amorous way
The Queen of No-land us'd to make thee King
Of her and hers (Oh) many a precious thing.
Thy London widdow next in love half drown'd,
Which thou refus'dft with forty thoufand pound :
Thy daunting Effex in his rafh bravado,
Raleigh's hard fcaping of thy baftinado :
Laftly, thy grace with thy great Queen Eliza,
Who, hadft thou had the learning to fuffice a
Man, but to write and rea i, had made thee able
To fit in Councell at her Highnefs Stable.
Thefe trophees of thy Fame, and myriads more
Kept by thy fertile brain for time in ftore,
I leave unfung, and wifh they may be writ
In golden lines by fome more happy wit,
Whofe Genius, till fome fury do h infpire,
Let me fit down in filence, and admire.

                                       A

THE END

Et him that undertook to praife
The French Pox, and fo many wayes
prove that it is now a days
                     Commodious :

y, let him a while give place,
I will prove, a fiery face
o the owner no difgrace,
                     Nor odious.

o hath a fiery face, that man
aid to have a rich face, and
bies about his nofe, none can
                     Deny it.

d all men know as well as I,
at what is rich, moft eagerly
covet, and no coft deny
                     To buy it.

ne have their clothes fold from their back,
d fome their lands, and fome will lack
at, rather than good fherry Sack
                     And Claret :

d they fwear (& fwear truth) that thofe
ich drink fmall beer, & wear good clothes,
offer wrong unto their nofe,
                     And marre it.

n Romes Senate long-nos'd men
e chofe for wifeft, tell me then
w thefe fhould not be praifed, when
                     All men know

A fiery face nere is without
A rich nose : and how far a snowt
Thats rich exceeds a long to doubt
                    Or call men to

Dispute or to capitulate,
This matter's not so intricate
But any may expostulate
                    And judge it :

And if judge truly hee'l confess,
Fire rich, exceeds long wise ; I guess.
No man that hath true worthiness
                    Will grudg it.

Besides, the world knows this that we
Affirm those gracious that we see.
But blush and call it modesty
                    In people.

A rich face always blushes, so
It doth all faces else out go
As far as St. Faiths is below
                    Pauls steeple.

He that reads this, and does not say,
A fiery face hath won the day,
In judgment shews himself a boy,
                    And heedless.

Nor will I spend more words to show
What commendation men do ow
To Captain Iones his face you know
                    Tis needless.

FINIS.

THE
EGEND

OF

Captain *JONES*:

CONTINUED

om his firſt part to his end :

WHEREIN IS DELIVERED

; incredible adventures and atchievements by
ea and land.

Particularly,

s miraculous deliverance from a wrack at Sea
by the ſupport of a Dolphin.

; ſeveral deſperate duels.

; combate with *Bahader Cham,*a Gyant of the
race of *Og.*

s loves.

s deep imployments, and happy ſucceſs in buſineſs of State.

*l which, and more, it but the tithe of his own relation,
which he continued untill he grew ſpeechleſs, and died.*

LONDON,

nted by *E.O.* for *Francis Haley,* and are to be ſold
at his Shop, at the upper end of *Chancery*
lane, next *Holborn,* 1670.

To the READER.

R Eader, *read on : here* you *may happ'ly meet*
  News, pleasing more, than what's cry'd in
                              (*your street.*

ones *is reviv'd ; were start : the danger's past ;*
hat he hath done long since, now makes him last
his last brave actions never sung before
'e offer to your view, nor write we more
han he made good on oath : then (pray) believe
hat here you'l find : thus by your faith he'l live.
Text, spare your censure on his Poets style ;
Had it gone high, his ghost had kept a quoile
'o be surmounted : down-right were his blows ;
'own-right his speech ; down-right to's grave he
                              (*goes*

nely his fame by your opinion may
Make him still live, though now he's dust or clay.

D 4   THE

THE
LEGEND
OF
Captaine *JONES.*

Continued from his first Part to his end.

WIll nothing please the taste of these rough
(times
at Rue and VVormwood stuft in Prose or Rimes?
o verse to make our Poets Laureate
at smart Iambicks lashing King or *State?*
inst all turn Mercuries, these times to fit
y poysoning Fame with their quick-silver wit?
hat name that's got by some notorious ill,
nd merits gives, is hateful to our quill.
ut if the last brave acts of Captain *Jones*
Which can move mirth and fear, and break no bones,
Iay be admitted in this ruffling age,
ehold him here re-mounted on our stage.

Ye

Yet know we still are ty'd to our low ttrein,
VVe muft not once tranfcend his down-right vein.
And if you meet ought favouring of a lye,
(Reader believe't) 'tis *Iones* that fpeaks, not I.
VVe left him priz'd on change, too dear 'twas thought
Twenty four Donns, & all not worth a groat, 24 *Spani*
Compar'd to him, though each had had cõmãd *comman-*
Over great Armies, preft for fea and land. *ders give*
Here fee him fhipt for his dear native coaft *in exchang*
VVhere ere he comes you'l find he'l rule the *s for him.*
                                        (roaft
VVith new found foes, who attempt his force to fhake
But fleeping Lions 'tis not wife to wake.
Now once more *Neptune* doth his waves inlarge,
Swoln big with pride, that Fate had giv'n him charge
And weighty convoy of this mighty man
To whence he came ; but ere the fhip had ran
Ten glaffes out, comes Boreas with a cloud
As black as ink ; the fteeres-man cries aloud
Down with the top-faile, keep the fprit-faile tight,
Haile the main bowling. Whilft this mask of light
Ufher'd with lightning plowes the angry deep
High as her felf in ridges, and as fteep
As *Cair*'s tall Pyramids ; the labouring fhip
Like a chaf'd Bear with Maftives, ftrives to keep
Her beak aloft ; fome billows fhe breaks throw,
Others mount over her at poop and prow.
Iones heard this ftir unmov'd : from *Neptune* ftill
He hop'd no good, nor ever fear'd his ill.
Thus whilft the carefull fea-men work and pray,
He carelefs to his cabbin calis his boy, And

nd makes him read to him the ancient stories
)f our old Englifh VVorthies, and their glories;
low our S. *George* did the fell Dragon gore ,
he like atchievement of Sir *Eglemore* :
opas hard queft after th'elf-queen to *Barwick*: *Sir Topas*
.e *Bvis* cow,& *Guy*'s fierce boar of *Warwick*: *rime in Chaucer.*
'hefe ftories read, exalt his haughty mind
.bove the fervile fear of fea or wind.
'he fhips hard ftate grew now from ill to worfe :
;etweẽ two hideous feas acrofs her courfe,
Ier whole bulk groans: her beak and main maft break.
hook with this fhock, fhe fprings a dangerous leak:
'Vhich her flye foe foon finds, and to begin
.ike a dire dropfie, drenches all within.
'hus whilft a treacherous in-mate fills her womb,
he's forc'd to be her own deftructions tomb.
.nd overburthen'd with what bore her before,
he's down-right foundred, and can work no more,
Iere might be feen the fad effects of feare
'Vhich feveral wayes in feveral men appear :
ome cry'd, fome pray'd, whilft others fwear or rave,
'o leave the land to make the fea their grave.
oner fwoln with the brave actions of his Knights,
;ig as the fea, afcends, and *Neptune* cites
'o fingle combate : when a boifterous wave
'Vhich *Neptune* fent to make him *Neptunes* flave,
'Vhurles him a cables length to fea, the fhip
inks with the reft, who give this world the flip.
'Vell now, Sir J*ones*, 'tis time to fhew your skill ;
fou muft fwim ftoutly for't, or drink your fill.

No

No danger frights thee, thou brave man of merit,
Thy body is boy'd up by thy blow'n spirit.
As a grim sea-calf still presaging storms
VVallows and wantons in cold Thetis arms :
Juſt ſuch is *Iones* : as if he had been bred
VVith her finn'd frie within her watry bed.
No ſhip for help, no land for hope appears;
Horror of billowes roaring in his ears.
Nothing ſupports but confidence alone, as
If ſome preſt VVhale muſt take up *Iones* like *Ionas*.
At laſt (alaſs!) he finds he is no fiſh,
His ſpirit 'gins to leave his treacherous fleſh.
Continual labouring makes his limbs wax ſtark
And ſtiff with cold, his optick ſenſe grows dark,
Neptune inſults, and brandiſhing his mace
Makes his rude billows daſh him ore the face.
Now ſee the fate of noble reſolution,
VVhen *Iones* thought nothing but of diſſolution,
Man's conſtant friend a gentle Dolphin glides
Between his thighes, on whom he mounts and
                                        (rides
In poſt with mighty ſpeed, through wind and
                                        (weather;
So his kind fiſh holds out he cares not whither;
Like a bold Centaur bravely he curvets
From ridge to ridge; twas ſtrange, how faſt he ſits
In this rough road; but *Iones* learn'd from his cradle
To ride without a ſtirrop or a ſaddle,
VVhen on the mountain tops wilde mares he ſpide,
He ſuckt them dry, and then ſtraight up and ride.

At

Alway portending ſtorms when they are ſeen to play.

The Dolphin is always obſerv'd to be a lover of man.

At laſt at this high ſpeed he gets the ſight
Of land, ſo neer, hee's ready to alight,
VVhen his kind fiſh much griev'd to leave the burthen
She lov'd ſo well, to ſea again doth turn
VVith mighty ſpeed, ſtill *Iones* doth her beſtride
Believing now he ſhould to th'Indias ride.
Fain would he turn her, but he knew not how,
He never knew a bridles want till now :
At laſt the faithful fiſh preferring higher
HerRiders ſafety then her own deſire,
She turns her courſe about with happy haſte,
And ſo our errant Knight on land ſhe caſt.
Some Spaniſh writers flatly do deny
He ſuffer'd wrack, and plainly term't a lye :
They ſay the ſhip that led this dangerous dance
Was built by *Lewis* King *Henry's* ſon of *France*,
And took that name from him, who bears *The eldeſt*
(that name *ſon of the*
As eldeſt ſon, who ſtill is ſty'ld the ſame : *King of*
They write *Jones* got this ground t'augment *France al-*
his glory *ways ſtiled*
And cheat the world with this ſtupendious *the Dol-*
(ſtory ; *phia.*

But let theReader judge if this be true,
And know pale envy ſtill doth worth purſue.
VVell, now to *Jones* again, we may conceive
He was not ill apaid to take his leave
Of this rough element : nor did accou t it
Much worſe to go on foot, then ride ſo mounted.
'Tis true, he road this lofty fiſh in ſtate,

D

But 'twas too neer the boisterous fit of Fate,
He fear'd not Fortune nor her wheel, though fickle,
Yet loth he was to be laid up in pickle ;
Or that his manly limbs should be a feast
For sharks, or crabs, or congers to digest.
His next work is to find some habitation,
Though he came safely there, 'twas in mean fashion,
The self-same clothes which when *Alonso* brav'd him,
He made him wear, and to the gally slav'd him.
And though this last foul storm had little harm'd him,
It seem'd to some strage thing to have transform'd him; *Nebuchad-*
Rigid and rough, long wet and feltred locks, *nezzar.*
Like *Babels* King, when turn'd into an Oxe :
For a fresh water soldier none could doubt him,
The seas salt tears ran trickling round about him.
In this cold plight he leaves the beachy strand,
And coasts the main with many a weary stand.
At last hespies a house, not great, but good :
For here he finds a brother of his brood,
Who had adventur'd in those ways before,
And rais'd some fortune by't, and gave it ore.
He quickly finds that *Jones* had scap'd some wrack ;
Experience, charity, and pity spake
On this behalf ; the good man bids him in,
And with *Y'are kindly welcome* doth begin.
He spak't in Dutch, which gladded *Jones*, for he *The same*
Could speak't as wel as *Grace dw worth awhee* . *in Welch.*
Which language a Dutch Pilot well had taught him.
When *Greenfield* to *America* had brought him,
By this, the Stove's made ready, in goes *Jones* :

                                        Dryes

ents, comforts nerves and bones.
homely wholesome chear,
pleat, strong Lubeck beere.
is mate: more fat then fair,
ind thereto debonaire.
sk what Country 'twas that gave
to her humble slave?
he Netherlands; the States
here many broken pates
and for his wants supply
wn of *Flushing* stood fast by,
rrice did command in chief
, and the States relief.
ith joy; for *Horace Vere*,
been (I know not where)
ere *Jones* did entertain
ith *Cumberland*, for *Spain*.
well, to take some rest
st directs his weary guest:
s fill, he timely rose,
ful leave, and on he goes.
ce his passage over
finds: from thence to *Dover*.
he resolves to touch,
d, the Bulwark of the Dutch,
s nis troop; here *Jones* arrives,
n Jaile, except his Gives,
be of Fryers gray,
o company, but they
im whilst he hath a rag; *Lowsie.*

Such

Such as poſſeſs the Begger with his bag.
Winds, ſtorms, nor ſeas, nor ought that could undo h
Could make them flinch, like friends they ſtick cloſ
(h

And thus accompanied he doth approach
To th'Generalls houſe, neither with ſteed nor coach
But in his manly foot-march : 'twas the time
When *Norrice* with his Chiefs were ſet to dine.
Jones preſſeth to the Parlor from the Hall,
And there accoſts the noble General.
Who ey'd him quickly, and cryes out (o fate!)
Live I to ſee the ſtrength of England's State?
Breath'ſt thou brave man at arms? *Jones* art thou he
On is it *Mars* himſelf diſguiſ'd like thee?
Quoth *Jones*. The ſcourge of Spaniards and of *Spai*
Whom they have felt and foyl'd, but to their pain,
Stands here ; and yet would breathe ſome few yea
To prove King *Philip* or my ſelf the ſtronger. (long
The reſt was dear embraces, and his place
By *Norrice* ſide ; and then a haſty grace.
Now might I dwell upon the luſcious chear,
Which here grew cold, whil'ſt each mans eye and e
Fed on the perſon and diſcourſe of *Jones*,
And quite forgot their toaſts and marrow bones.
And whilſt his ſtrange adventures paſt, he tells ;
The Captains, Serjeant-Majors, Collonels
Faſt to adm're him, and are fill'd with wonder,
And feel no hunger though their bellies thunder.
Here mark his conſtancy, beyond theſe men.
He eats and talks, and eats and talks agen.

The

Their mawes are cloy'd to hear thofe deeds of his,
His ftories are his meals Parenthefis.
But when he fpoke of Spain, 'tis paft belief,
What fearful wounds he gave the chine of beef.
A capon garnifh'd with flic'd lemmons ftood
Before him, which he tore as he were wood ;
And made it leglefs ere he made a paufe,
Meerly in malice to the Spanifh fawce.
He wrecks his wrath on every difh that's nigh him,
And fpoil'd a cuftard that ftood trembling by hmi ;
Grow'n pikes and carps, and many a dainty difh,
That far excell'd his tame Crotonian fifh.
At laft his fury 'gan to be affwag'd,
And then the General all his friends ingag'd,
To give him Souldiers welcome in a rowfe
Of lufty Rhenifh, till both men and houfe
Turn round. Once two great deities conjoyn'd
To work his fall, with hideous feas and wind :
Now onely Bacchus takes the man to task ;
And layes fore at him with his potent cask.
And whilft with lufty grape ore-born *Jones* reels,
H'affaults his head, and fo trips up his heels.
But up he rofe again with vigour ftout,
And fwears, though foil'd, hee'l try another bout.
They all were now high flow'n, when Collonel Skink
Fills a huge bowl of fherry Sack, to drink
A health to Englands Queen, and *Jones* is he
Muft tak't in pledge ; and fo he did : but fee
The ftrange antipathy between this man
And Spanifh grape, as well as Spanifh Don.

E   Againft

Againſt them both his ſtomach fierce doth riſe,
No ſooner drunk, but up again it flies.
Th s odd diſtemper made him half aſham'd,
But there's no help, he was with wrath inflam'd ;
Nor was he pleas'd with Skink for this affront,
(For ſo he took't) he knew Skink could not want
The wine of Rhene for healths : why then in Sack,
Unleſs it were to lay him on his back?
Fir'd with this thought, he catcht at his buff-coat,
Then grapples cloſe ; and had pluckt out his throat,
But that the wary General interpoſes
His hands and friends between their bloody noſes :
And with ſtrong reaſons, ſmiles, and ſmooth allyes,
He damps the fury of theſe fiery boyes,
And left them (as he thought) well reconcil'd,
But by th' effect he found he was beguil'd.
The night diſpers'd them now to ſeveral wayes,
As they were quarter'd. *Jones* with *Norrice* ſtayes,
Who ſent him the next morn a brave rich ſuit,
Intended for himſelf, with all things to't.
Scant was he dreſs'd, when Skink unto him ſerds
A Captain, boldly to demand amends
For laſt nights work; and *Jones* to do him right,
A bullet muſt exchange in ſingle fight.
For which himſelf and Second would not miſs,
Where *Jones* deſign'd to meet with him and his.
This *Jones* accepts, and ſwears before that night
He ſhall hear from him, how, and where he'l figh:
He thus diſpatcht, Sir *Roger Williams* enters,
To whom much kind diſcourſe paſt ore ; he venters

To tell his difference with Skink; which told,
Sir Roger like a Britain true and bold,
Protects himself his Second, hasts to Skink,
Tells him, h' had need fight well, as well as drink:
That *Jones* and he at the South-postern gate
Early next morn would meet him and his mate,
With sword and pistol hors'd, and there agree
To fight it two to two, or *Jones* and he.
Then comes to *Jones*, supply'd him with a horse
Well rid and fierce; Bucquoy had felt his force
Before Breda; then gives that sword and belt
Which Prince Llewellin wore, when slain near *The Prince*
                        (Bealt. *of South-*
The hour come, these champions soon appear, *Wales,*
They spend no time in words; in full career, *who was*
Jones charges bravely close up to his brest, *slain near*
And fires, but fortune turn'd it to the best: *Bealt, a*
Makes him through haste forget to prime his *Town in*
                           (pan, *Brecknock-*
                                shire.
So mist his shot, and so preserv'd the man.
Vext with this faile, he flings with all his might,
Worse than the bullet, had his hand gone right,
His pistol at his face; 'twas aim'd so near,
It raz'd his cheek, and took quite off his ear.
Skink's bullet pierc'd the bow of *Jones* his saddle,
And slightly circumcis'd his foremans noddle:
The Second stood attending the event
Of this first charge, both resolutely bent,
If either in th' incounter had been sped,
To run the same adventure they both did.
              E 2

But when they faw the bravery of their fight,
Both having loft their blood, the quarrel flight:
They both deteft fuch men fhould be deftroy'd,
By which their countrey fhould be fore annoy'd:
With joynt confent their power they unite
To ride up to them, and break off the fight:
Thus got between them, all beft means they ufe
To take it up; which both inrag'd refufe.
They urge the equal terms on which they ftood,
In point of honour: both had loft their blood,
Both fought it well; how light their quarrels ground,
Not worth one drop of blood, much lefs a wound.
Then bid them look on their dear countries woe,
Whofe breafts muft fuffer for the ill they doe.
Reafon takes place of wrath, they both accord,
And mifchiefs engine refts: they fheath the fword.
And thus (in few) this dangerous duel ends,
Fierce foes they met, and now return good friends:
Their Surgeons ftanch their blood, for yet they bled,
And clap a cap on *Jones* his nether head.
This news comes quickly to the Generals ear,
Who when he heard their lives were out of fear,
He gently chides them that they would expofe
Their limbs unto the various chance of blows
In fingle duel, when the common good
No longer ftands then fuch good members ftood.
Ten dayes are fpent ere *Jones* could ftand upright,
Through his flight hurt: which come, the noble
(Knigh

Brave

Brave *Norrice* he takes leave of, with the rest
Of that brave martial crew, and then addrest
Himself for *England* : Joy thou happy Isle,
Thy Son returns that hath kept all this quoile :
Ye blustering boyes of Britain feast and quaff all :
The man's at hand whose presence makes you laugh all.
Welcome to Dover thou great son of Mavors,
So spake the Mayor of Dover on his grave horse,
Mounted to meet him with his reverend train,
All gown, who cry him welcome home from Spain.
After some short repast, on post he rides
To Non-such, where her Majesty resides,
Where he was soon brought up to kiss her hand,
By his dear friend, *George* Earl of Cumberland.
But then when took to private conference,
What news of moment, what intelligence,
What Spanish plots, what mysteries of state,
Into her Majesty he did relate,
Twas wrapt in clouds too high for me to know it ;
Then pardon, Reader, that I do not show it.
But 'twas observ'd he gave a written book
Into her hand : on which she deign'd to look,
And seem'd to slight it in the publique face
Of Court, yet made some use of 't in a place
That's privy, so dismist him to his rest,
Or her Courts welcome ; as to him seem'd best.
Twas now the time when * *Essex* was in-   * Robert
                             (gag'd *Earl of*
In Ireland 'gainst *Tyrone* , with whom he *Essex.*
                           (wag'd

A bloody war : which to the Queen and state
Seem'd long and costly : after much debate,
It is resolv'd to pick out such a man,
Whose active force and spirit dares and can
Put a full period to this war at once,
Without delay, and this was Captain *Jones*,
On whom they pitch, who fed on hopes in vain
To get some small command to conquer Spain.
'Tis first resolv'd he must reduce Tyrone,
Till that be done he must let Spain alone.
Thus his Commission's seal'd to raise his force,
A compleat Regiment of British horse :
He's thence to waft them ore the Irish brine ;
And then his force with noble Essex joyn.
Jones lost no time, goes in five dayes to VVales :
Shews his commission, tells them glorious tales ;
He need not beat a drum, nor sound a trumpet,
His name's enough to make these Britains jump' at
This brave employment under such a Chief,
VVhose fame's reserve enough for their relief.
Perplext he was in choosing his Commanders,
For he still fancied best his old Highlanders ;
But many worthies of the lower parts,
Offer to him their fortunes and their hearts.
But all respects put by, h' inlisteth ten
Of his old gang, all hard-bred mountain-men
For his Life-guard, Thomas Da Price a Pew,
Jenkin Da Prichard, Evan David Hugh,
John ap John Jenkin, Richard John dap Reese,
And Tom Dee Bacgh, a fierce Rat at green cheese,

L'e-

Llewelling Reefe ap David, VVatkin Jenkin,
VVith Howell Reefe ap Robert, and young Philkin;
Thefe for his guard, his Officers in chief,
Lieutenant Collonel Craddock, a ftout thief,
VVith Major Howell ap Howell of Pen Crag,
VVell known for plundering many a cow and nag,
Captain Pen Vaure, a branch of Tom John Catty,
Whofe word in's colours was, *TE ROGUES have at ye.*
Griffith ap Reefe ap Howel ap Coh ap Gwillin.
Reefe David Shone ap Ruthero ap VVilliam,
VVith many more whofe names 'twere long to write,
The reft their acts will get them names in fight.
VVe muft conceive they all were men of fame,
For here we fee them all men of great name.
Jones with thefe blades advanceth to the *dale,   * *A little*
There lines himfelf and them with noble Ale   *village by*
Of fuch antiquity as hath not been there   *Milford.*
The like fince * Robert of the Vale was feen * *An old*
                          (there.   *Welch Pro-*
VVho us'd to fink thofe kinterkins of merit,   *phet, who*
To raife the heat of his prophetick fpirit.   *foretold*
His forces flipt, at laft aboard he goes;   *the landing*
A lufty South-eaft gale fo fairly blows,   *of Henry*
That forty hours eafily brought him in   *the feven'h*
To Dubline Harbor where he lands his men;   *there.*
There getting knowledge where the Army lay,
To the Lord General he takes his way;
From whom a noble welcome he receives,
And good frefh quarter to his troops he gives.

Jones first informs himself in what condition
Tyron's made up for war, what ammunition,
How fortifi'd in camp, what force, what watch,
How victuall'd, all occasion he doth catch
To take him tripping ; when at length he found,
He would not give nor take on equal ground,
To hazard battel, he resolves to try him
In such a way as he should not deny him,
Unless with loss of honour ; he indites
This fearful challenge, which his Squire writes :
False traytor to thy country and thy Queen,
I he who yet my peer have never seen
In feats of arms, whose martial hand hath slain
Kings with their armies, half unpeopl'd Spain :
Done more than I can write ; I say, I he
Urge thee to single duel : and to thee
Give thee free choice of weapon, time, and place,
On foot or horse-back : think it no disgrace,
That I a private Captain, thou a Chief,
(My deeds make me admir'd, thee thine a thief)
Call thee to question, 'twere ambition
In thee, to hope to fall by such a one,
T' augment my praise I wish thee five times stronger,
Live till I meet thee, and but little longer,
This done, a Herauld is straight charged with it,
In publique to Tyron's own hand to give it,
Who to him hastes, and in the publique view
Of all his Army sayes (Tyrone) to you
I have command to bring from Captain *Jones*
This challenge ; read it, and resolve at once.

: takes it, reads it, and admires the man
at sends him this high Brave, who if he can
it half he writes, he counts himself but lost,
meet him ; yet in sight of all his host
his Brave was giv'n him : thus his honour lyes
t stake, he therefore desperately replyes.
ell your brave man I am not conquer'd yet,
or can by words but blows, he shall be met,
efore to morrow noon, on yon green plot,
rrounded with the bog, neither with shot,
or head-steel'd dart : this sword I wear shall do't,
rm'd cap-a-pe, no horse, but foot to foot.
e thus dispatcht, Tyrone doth straight seek out,
ryan Mac-kill-cow a strong sturdy lout,
ade up with nerves, and brawn and bone so mighty,
e felt no burden were it ne're so weighty.
he strongest man in all his camp by half,
ilo's great bull to him was but a calf.
red in the Irish wildes 'mongst bogs and woods,
nd like an out-law liv'd on others goods.
nd this was he on whom Tyrone now fixt,
o personate himself in fight betwixt
im and our *Jones*, true arms of largest size
e donns on him, then to his loyns he tyes
orglay his trusty sword, then swears devoutly,
f in this combat he behave him stoutly ,
e'l raise his means above two English Barons,
n lands, and sheep, and cows, and lusty garrons :
ryan's all confidence, and hastens thither,
Where *Jones* and he must try their force together,

The

The place defign'd was hardly twelve yards fquare,
No traverfing of ground, no boys-play there,
The reft was bog, ore which fome planks were laid
To pafs them ore ; and then, to ftop all aid,
Were took from thence : here *Jones* our valiant fighte
Advanceth firft : Bryan with his fell fmiter
Is hard at hand, they fpare no time for words,
Their mettal is the whetftone of their fwords.
They clap together like two fons of thunder,   (unde
The blades ftruck lightning, whilft the earth quak'
The burthen fhe bore; no ftroke that's given, but deat
Seems to attend it, till both out of breath,
Confent to make a ftand, but this fhort reft
Was like a fallet with a muttons breft
To their fharp ftomacks, to't they go again,
And lay on load like devils, not like men.
Their well-try'd arms do blufh with their own blood,
To find their flefh in whofe defence they ftood,
Stand, whilft it fell : for that their keen fwords whipt of
As it they would each other make a chipt loaf.
At laft, as I have feen a man of war
Exalt a Carrick, which exceeds him far,
In bulk and ftrength : fo *Jones* deals now with Bryan,
Who fhuns and fhifts, more like a Fox than Lyon.
For (to fpeak truly) this fell Pagan lout
Doth fo belabour *Jones* from head to foot,
That both his ears do o't with forrow fing,
And's eyes fee ftars at noon (a wondrous thing)
We muft conceive thofe furious blows he dealt,
Were well repaid with ufe, which Bryan felt.

But

t *Jones* esteeming it an equal thing
he self-conquer'd, and long conquering,
solves to put the business out of doubt
ith one Pass more, which was the fatal bout.
n this Resolve, with both his hands he prest
e pummel of his sword against his brest,
en like a thunder-bolt tilts swiftly at him:
ith th' fear of this, Bryan had quite forgot him,
hat 'twas a bog behind, so backward springs,
nd his whole body up to th' arm-pits flings,
midst the bog. *Jones* driven with his own force,
ssing his thrust falls headlong in the gorse,
ut pitcht upon his foe, by happy fate,
With which ore-born, our *Jones* so mauls his pate,
that th' helmet flees, and leaves his head to th' danger,
f being the anvil of our *Jones* his anger:
nd now the day is his, his strength he strains
With hand and hilt to beat out Bryans braits:
Who cries out quarter, Man of Mars I yield
My self and sword, the honour of the field.
nd where the power rests, 'tis much better far
o give than take a life in chance of war.
his and the bog doth cool the wrath of *Jones*,
He spares his life, and draws him forth at once.
esides, he scorn'd posterity should tell,
hat by his hand Tyrone s' ignobly fell.
nd thus Oneale his captive (as he thought)
n this foul plight unto the camp he brought:
resents him to the General, and then spake,
r, if you have ten more Tyrones to take,

Command,

Command, Ile do't; here fee him hither led
By me, who all this charge and ftir hath bred.
The joy was great, but fhort ; 'twas quickly known,
This was but fome impoftor from Tyrone :
And this an Irifh Captive at firft view
Made known, who him and his condition knew.
This bred a qualm in fome, whilft others fmil'd
To fee their Britifh Champion fo beguil'd,
And that Tyrone had bobb'd him with this jeer,
To match his Cow-herd with our Mountaineer.
Jones vext with this, retires unto his tent,
An angry, dirty, defperate, male-content.
Three dayes thus fpent, his wrath no longer bears
This bafe affront ; (like Scævola,) he fwears   *Scævola*
He'l kill Tyrone in midft of all his force,   *againft*
Though in the act himfelf be made a coarfe :   *Porfenna,*
                                                                      in Livit.
In this wild mood by night he doth convey
Himfelf where he fuppos'd the Rebell lay :
Who wifely rais'd his camp the day before,   (more
March'd far through defart woods, and would no
Of thefe affronts ; which to put off agen
Might breed contempt of him with his own men.
Two dayes *Jones* fpends in quefts to find him out ;
At laft he was encountred with a rout
Of ravening wolves, who fiercely all at once
Affail'd the back and face of manly *Jones.*
'Twas time to draw, elfe thefe wild Irifh dogs
Had been fo bold to fhake him by the logs :
But when his fword was out he makes them feel,
Their teeth are not fo fharp as his true fteel.

The

ıe firſt good blow he dealt took off a head,
ıe ſecond made one two ; the next he ſped,
'ith a ſore thruſt at mouth, and out at tail :
ǀfourth with his poſteriors doth aſſail,
'ith his ſtrong heel he hurles againſt a tree
ǀvelve paces from his kick, and there lyes he :
ǀis ſword rips up anothers empty paunch ;
ıe next limps off from him with half a haunch.
'e muſt conceive 'twas time to lay about him,
ǀor here were thoſe that ſought to eat, not rout him.
ǀor ſcap'd he free, the rich ſword-skarf he wore
ǀbout his loyns, they all to fitters tore.
ǀis boots pluckt off by bits, ſome fleſh to boot,
ǀo quarter free from ſcars from head to foot.
ǀıd (to conclude) from theſe wild Iriſh *Lupanthro-*
ǀ   (witches *pos, Witches*
ǀe ſcapes ſcant with a hands breadth of his *that take*
ǀ   (breeches. *ſhapes of*
ǀǀearied with blows and kicks, at laſt they *Wolves up-*
ǀ   (fly him, *Ireland.*
ǀnd take a ſnarling leave as they go by him.
ǀhus *Jones*, half worried, haſtes unto the camp,
ǀhere's none could ſay the cloathes he wore were
ǀ   (damp
ǀith night perdues, unleſs they meant to flout him ;
ǀor (to ſpeak truth) he had no cloathes about him.
ǀhus come, he ſwears by the immortal powers,
ǀe had maintain'd a battel full five houres,
ǀith forty duels, five and twenty kill'd,
ǀouted the reſt ; who all had took the field

'Gainſt

'Gainft him alone ; all rais'd with him to fight,
To his deftruction, or t'eclipfe his might,
By that old timerous, treacherous kern Tyrone,
Who durft as well meet death as him alone.
The plight our *Jones* appear'd in, made none doubt
But he had had at leaft a devilifh bout,
If not with Devils ; on him each man feeth
The fearful character of nails and teeth.
We may not ftand to fhew what Effex's fence
Was on thefe actions, nor the confequence
They did import : the progrefs of this ftory
Haftens our Mufe to *Jones* his farther glory.
Fame thefe atchievements brings to Englands State ;
Which held the Queen and Council in debate
About this man ; and all at laft fuppos'd,
In policy he's not to be expos'd
To the clofe dangerous plots of fuch a foe,
Who neither values faith nor honour, fo
His mifchiefs take fuccefs ; and thus the State
Lofe this dear Limb, and then repent too late.
Some looking deeper into *Jones* his fpirit,
Knowing he knew too much of his own merit,
Held it not fafe he fhould be open to
The windy baits of that fo fubtile foe,
To gain him to his part ; whofe haughty mind
Would foon take fire ; then could not be confin'd.
And if by fuch a plot they fhould be croft,
They all conclude that Kingdom were quite loft.
Thefe grounds invite them wholly to decline
His warfare there ; fo on fome grand defign

etended they invite his quick repair
Englands Court, to act this great affair.
e comes, but leaves his British troops to fight
rone to death ; whose acts who please to write,
ay meet with subjects brave to rant upon,
it for my self, I am quite tyr'd with one.
d thus transported from the Irish strands,

 Aberust with a VVelch Port he lands ; *A Town*
Vhere ere two dayes he fully spent for rest, *and Port*
goodly vessel with cross winds opprest, *in the*
mes boyling in; *Jones* by her colours knows *County of*
e is of Spain : his colour comes and goes *Cardigan.*
sight of hers ; that such a goodly prey,
ould come (as 'twere) to meet him in his way.
e musters strait a troop of british lads,
Vho on their mountain geldings clapt their pads ;
Vith rusty bills instead of staves in rest ;
ch were their horse, such were their arms at best,
en with a fowling-piece the ship they hail,
Vith confidence that she would straight strike sail :
it she makes answer, that she was too hot,
om her broad side with twenty Culverin shot.
is struck a stand, till *Jones* cry'd out, what doubt ye ?
e day is ours, my masters lay about ye,
ad the forlorn up bravely, and be bold,
 bring the rear, for they know me of old ;
once my name or person they descry,
y life for yours, they'l either yield or fly.
ade bold with this, in full carreer they ride
to the ridges of the flowing tide.

         The

But when they came breſt-high amongſt the waves,
Their horſe more wiſe by half then theſe mad knaves
Snort at the foaming billows, turn their tails,
And make a fair retreat from Sea and Sails ;
Which leſt it ſhould ſeem done on terms of fear,
Jones to the front now haſtens from the rear,
And leads them back again in good array,
Neither with haſty flight, nor much delay.
At his return he ſearcheth all that coaſt,
To find a herring-boat, or two at moſt ;
With which he doubts not but he'l ſink or take
This luſty Ship ; whoſe braveſt men will quake
To hear his name. But fate that had decreed
To ſave her, caus'd her hoyſe her ſails with ſpeed ;
So with a ſtrong fore-wind away ſhe flyes,
And leaves our *Jones* to ſeek ſome other prize.
Thus croſt in his deſign, to Court he went,
Where he is met with noble complement ;
And from the Queen ſuch grace he doth receive,
As he deſerv'd, and ſtood with her to give.
Now for the great affair that call'd him back,
The Lords muſt pump for't in a cup of Sack
To help invention : *Jones* muſt be preferr'd
To ſome imployment, be it nere ſo hard.
In deep conſult and long diſcourſe they ſat on't,
And ſtudied for't ; at laſt they lighted pat on't.
It is reſolv'd, that he muſt be the man
 To go in embaſſy to Preſter John.
The buſineſs carried with't a glorious face ;
Employ'd embaſſador unto his Grace.

he dangerous voyage to a place remote,
ffects him most to get his name more note
ı forreign Lands ; he'l not refuse the work,
Vere't to the Great *Mogul* , or the Great *Turk.*
. lusty Ship's prepar'd, again he goes ;
ut what this great imployment was, who knows?
eader, I know thy thoughts are strongly bent
o know this first design, on which he went.
ut know this first, that Princes secret wayes
re such as Ships cut thorow deepest Seas,
Vhich shut still as they ope, and him that sounds
nd enters too far in, their deepness drowns.
bare conjectures may give light to thee,
lere take them freely ; harmless thoughts are free.
erhaps this high-blown spirit now is sent
o forreign air, where it may purge and vent,
nd so return more fit the State to serve
ı their commands, who yet must him observe.
erhaps he went this Priestly Prince to gain
nto our Church ; who gave good proof in *Spain*
f's power in this ; or to negotiate
ommerce between the *Ethiop* and our State,
ır tusks of Elephants to haft our knives,
pes, and Baboons, and Puggs, to please our wives ;
Vhich things satiety makes common there,
nd curiosity oprepriseth here.
e't what it will, our *Jones* is gone upon't,
nd we may know he will make something on't.
is treacherous friend, the Sea, his charge receives,
ıd with some flattering gales his hopes deceives,

F

Making

Making the Land, his firmer friend, appear
Still lefs; untill at laft it brought him where
He loft her fight: for three months time he makes
Good way; at laft the wind his wings forfakes;
The Ship's becalm'd, and for the Port fhe feeks,
She gains not half a league for thirteen weeks.
Jones finds this lazie war offends him more,
Then all thofe hideous ftorms out-rid before.
Thefe fad effects this fleepy calm attend,
Victual and beverage fpent; lefs hope of end.
Then fear of further miferies enfues,
The Sea with calms his patience doth abufe,
Turns devilifh States-man, puts on a fmooth face,
Salutes and kills them with a foft imbrace.
'Twas now far worfe with *Jones* then erft with *Skink*,
For three weeks his own Urine is his drink,
Which his hot body had fo oft fublim'd,
Tis grow'n a cordial, like gold thrice calcin'd.
Preefes of wind at laft his fails difplay,
And waft him into the Barbarick bay,
Then to the Arabick, next the Pilot laves
His boifterous charge in *Mare rubrum*'s waves,
And laftly, he attains, beyond all hope,
Errocco the fole Port of *Æthiope*;
And here he lands, and empties many a bowl
To allay the fury of his thirfty foul.
After fome reft he gets intelligence,
Where 'twas the Prince then kept his refidence:
Where he repairs, and's told when he comes thither,
The Prince and town are both remov'd together.

Some

ome ten miles off. The Prince and Town? (quoth
(*Jones*)

have met my match : here's people make no bones
Of things beyond belief. And yet 'was true ;
This town was tents which fifty thousand drew,
And rais'd in th'inftant wherefoere the Prince
ate down to fport, or fhew magnificence.
By Mount *Amara* now his Court he rears ;
A Mount far differing from the name it bears: *Read Pur-*
f Paradife had ere a fecond birth   *chas in his*
Below the feat of Saints, 'tis there on earth.   *relations*
in humble valley is the Garden where   *of Æthio-*
This Mount is rais'd ; a vale fo rich, fo rare ;   *pia, touc-*
Nature grew bankrupt drawing this rich plot; *ing this*
and ftriving to be quaint, fhe quite forgot   *Mount.*
o keep referves : for by this work we know,
he made it fuch fhe could make no more fo.
Amidft this vale is rais'd this lofty ftructure,
ive leagues upright. It's outfides architecture
Inpolifh'd Marble ; but fo rich, fo fair,
ou'd think't a pillar of one ftone in th'air,
y fome high power unto *Atlas* given,
o eafe his fhoulders whil'ft it proppeth Heaven.
his goodly Mount a fpecious plain doth crown,
nboft with Natures gemms, a velvet down
hat's always green ; no froft, no winter here,
ontinual Spring : here *Phœbus* all the year
rom rife to fet, doth always fire his eye,
s loath to put fo fair an object by.

F 2
Here

Here grow thofe happy trees from whence there
                                          (fpring

That precious oyl which erft anoynted Kings,
And facred Priefts. Nor croud they here to take
One fenfe alone ; the fcent and fight partake.
So they are rank'd, as well to give a grace,
As fweet perfumes, for tribute to the place.
No Orchard here, nor Garden, but the Plain,
The choiceft fruit all *Europe* doth contain,
Grow here unplanted, here's the lufcious Grape,
That makes *Joves* Nectar : 'twas not *Helens* rape
That ruin'd *Troy* : the Apple got from thence   *The Apple*
Had worth enough to do't. Here every fenfe   *which thre*
Would furfeit, but each objects rarity   *goddeffes,*
Gives appetite without fatiety :   *June, Pal-*
                                                 las, and
Rofes and Tulips *Flora* gathers here   (hair,   *Venus, co-*
When we have none, to crown her golden   *tended for*
And here *Medea* pickt (if *Jones* fpeak truth) *which wa*
Thofe herbs which turn'd antiquity to youth: *given by*
The only Phœnix deignes to weather here,   *Paris to*
The only place, like her, without a peer :   *Venus :*
Left all thefe fweets fhould want fweet har-   *whereupo*
                                       (mony,   *followed*
                                                 the deftru-
A numerous quire of Nightingales comply   *ction of*
To warble forth the fweet *Amara's* praife,   *Troy.*
Who turns their mourning notes to merry
                                        (layes.

Amidft this plain there glides a filver brook,
So gently, that the fubtil'ft eye may look,
And find no motion ; on his violet banks

                                          Thic

hick Cyprefs-trees marfhal themfelves in ranks,
o keep out Phœbus ; whofe inamour'd beams
eep through each little crink to view his ftreams :
lis pavement, azure gravel intermixt
Vith orient pearls, and diamonds betwixt;
Vhich, as the air's foft breath his furface purles,
ary their glofs, and twinkle through his curles :
ike a fteel'd glafs prefenting to the eye
he fpangled beauty of the ftarry sky.
lere Dolphins leave the fea to wanton ; here
arps fince the deluge their grown bodies cheer :
mbrana's too : fuch had * *Vitellius* known,   * *A great*
. Province fhould have gone to purchafe *Epicure, and*
                             (one : *Emperour*
                                    of Rome.
uch is *Amara*, fuch is *Tempe* field,
lyfium on earth unparalleld,
Twas here this royal Prieft now kept his Court :
place well fuiting with his fame and port.
nd here comes *Jones*, where having made's addrefs,
etters of credence given at his accefs,
n Latine writ : in the fame tongue he gives
ones gracious words ; which language Jones conceives
o be *Arabick*, for the Latine Tongue
He nere indur'd to learn nor old nor young.
But that's all one, there's no reply expected,
Into a rich pavilon he's directed
By men of State, where he is well attended,
With all that's rich, and to his reft commended.
ome few dayes fpent, and time for audience got,
When *Prefter John* in royal State was fet ;

Jones studying how t'expreſs his eloquence
In ſome ſtrange language which might poze the Prince,
Now trouls him forth a full-mouth'd Welch oration,
Boldly deliver'd as became his Nation.
The plot prov'd right, for not one word of ſence
Could be pickt from't, which vex'd the learned Prince.
His learned Linguiſts are call'd in to hear,
Who might as well have ſtopt each others ear
For ought they underſtood, and all proteſt
It was the very language of the Beaſt.
Jones hath his end, and then to make it known
He had more tongues t'expreſs himſelf than one;
In a new tone he ſpeaks, not half ſo rich,
But better known, 'twas *Engliſh*; unto which
An *Engliſh* Factor is Interpreter
Between our Captain and *John Presbyter*;
His buſineſs takes effect (what ere it was)
And great expreſſes of reſpect do paſs
To *Jones* from him, as one he thought moſt rich
In unknown tongues, expreſt in his firſt ſpeech,
And ſo admires him for he knows not what:
But *Jones* may thank his mother-tongue for that.
His buſineſs done, he's led, for recreation,
To take the pleaſures of that pleaſant Nation,
To Mount *Amara's* top, the chiefeſt grace,
And perfect beauty of that Kingdoms face;
And finding his great heart was moſt enclin'd
To Martial feats, all in one motion joyn'd
T'invite him to their Deſarts, where he might
Make trial of his force in manly fight

With

With their wild beasts, and promis'd him conforts
All truly try'd t'assist him in those sports.
The motion takes, a brave accoutred Horse,
And his own arms, he and's associate force
Advance to hunt; me thinks I see them all
Drawn to the life in canvasse*'gainst the wall,   * painted
In som mean house made for good-fellowship, *cloths in*
How fierce they look,how brave they prance *Inns and*
                (and skip ; *victualling houses.*

With hounds and horns, and bills, and pikes and
                         (glaves,
And spears, and clubs, and many light-foot knaves :
In this brave equipage they march away
To the known haunts where these wild creatures
                       (prey.

Twas *Jones* his trick of old to ride alone :
In hard adventures he'll admit of none
To share with him, from them he steals aside,
And in the desart by himself doth ride :
Nor rode he long till just against him stalks
A ramping Lion new come from his walks ;
Jones draws, the furious beast, with fiery eyes
And bristled mane, against his bosom flies:
But his keen sword met full with his fore paws,
And whipt them off ; and so he scap't his claws.
Nor staid it there, but gave a cruel wound
To his left jaw, and fell'd him to the ground.
Then nimbly wheels about, and stept aside,
Leaps from his horse, which to a tree he ty'd :
Then turns again, and with his sword falls to't,

To end this combate with him foot to foot,
The wounded beast with all his power doth hasten
His fearful fangs in *Jones* his throat to fasten.
Whilst on's hin feet he assaults him bolt upright,
With left hand arm'd, *Jones* stuns him with the right
Strikes both his hin legs off: yet on his stumps
The noble beast unconquer'd, fiercely jumps
Full at his face with open mouth, and there,
(For his grim face could raise in *Jones* no fear)
In shoots the deadly blade, and out behind,
Where't makes a second vent for lifes short wind ;
This thrust with right hand arm'd so home was sent,
That hand and hilt quite through together went:
Where taking hold of his strong stern (for truth
He swears) he drew't quite through his trunck this
                                                (mouth.
Then with fine force (the like was never seen)
He strips his inside out, and's outside in,
Thus tergiverst upon his steed he flings him,
Then mounts himself, and to the Court he brings him.
Never was Royal beast so grosly jaded,
But 'twas his face which could not be evaded:
Unto the gallants of the Court he shews
How hard th' adventure was, what thrusts, what blows;
On every circumstance he doth dilate ;
Nor adds he much to truth, nor much doth bate :
For what he spake, the Lyon made it good
With loss of his four legs, and his best blood.
This strang atchievement strikes them all with wonder,
'Twas never seen since *Greeces Alexander.*

                                                Lysima-

Lysimachus, Lisander, nor *Perdicas,*
Nor any of his Chiefs, ere did the like as
Our *Jones* in this : 'Tis true, they write they
                                    (kill'd,
In single fight, some few of these in field ;
But here's a force born with a higher sail,
Transporting tayl to head, and head to tayl.
The Prince in words this high atchievement prais'd :
But inward fear and jealousie it rais'd
Of our brave Queen, whose Scepter doth command
Such men whose power no Nation can withstand.
Jones might so far on his own strength presume, as
To seize his Throne, as * *Cortez Montezuma's*
Had done before. These thoughts he oft re-
                                    (volves
With troubled mind, and so in fine resolves
To shift him thence : makes for his fair pre-
                                    (tence,
Matter of high and hasty consequence,
To be with speed convey'd unto our Queen;
Except her self it must by none be seen.
This past on *Jones,* who parts with high content,
Nobly presented with fair complement.
Amongst the rest, a Parrot that could speak
All tongues but *Jones* his own ; that had a beak
Of perfect coral, plum'd as white as snow :
This he accepts, and so to sea doth go :
Where under sail such welcome he receives,
As one dire foe unto another gives.
With calms, and storms, and winds, all cross, that bear
                                    The

*Read Cur-
tius, touch-
ing these.*

* *A private
Spanish
Comman-
der, that
took this
great King
of Mexico
with a
handful of
men.*

The ſhip quite off the courſe that ſhe would ſteer.
Long time thus ſpent, into a Bay he drives,
And at a Port unknown at laſt arrives :
Where he beholds a glorious Caſtle built
High on a cliff, whoſe walls pure gold, or gilt
To him appear'd. Which object caus'd him land,
To know who did this Princely ſeat command.
He's told it is the Queen of *No-lands* place,
The onely Relict of her Royal race,
A Maiden Queen that here doth keep her Court,
Where many Kings, and Princes of high port
Make their addreſs, and loſe themſelves in love,
To purchaſe hers; for not a man can move
Her heart to wed, though nere ſo great his ſtate,
Or form exact, ſuch was the will of Fate.
Here as he lands, a large Cannow was ſent
To know from whence he was, and whither bent.
In this a Dutch-man came by happy Fate,
Who could his Language to the Queen tranſlate.
This man he tels, as briefly as he can,
His voyage from his Queen to *Preſter John* :
How by croſs winds in his return he's blown,
And forc'd into this port to him unknown.
Jones is reſolv'd to ſee, and to be ſeen
Of this great Princeſs, that our virgin Queen
Might know, when he returns, what form, what port
This Royal virgin carried in her Court.
Thus like an errant Knight all arm'd compleat,
He marcheth boldly to her Palace gate,
All maſſie poliſh'd braſs ; at his firſt ward,

ix milk-white Panthers fierce were chain'd for guard.
Thence through a large and fpecious Court he paft,
And fo afcends twelve Ivory fteps at laft,
With ebon columns, unto which were ty'd
Twelve fharp-kept Lyons, who all yawned wide
When ftrangers did approach. *Jones* through them
(all
s fafely guarded to a goodly Hall.
From thence afcends to rooms of greater ftate,
And comes at laft where th' Princefs Royal fate
Upon a ftrange rich bed, not ftuff'd with down,
But clofely wrought, and like a bladder blown;
Three *Æthiops* on each fide, to fan the air
With Oftridge plumes, perfum'd, as rich as fair.
Her beauty could not boaft of white and red,
But jet-like black; about her crifp curl'd head
And cheeks, there hang rich flaming ftones and pearls,
That paft *Mark Anthony's* *Ægyptian* girls.
In brief; if *Tufcan* liv'd to limne the night
Sparkling with ftars, this were her picture right.
No fooner in her fight doth *Jones* appear,
Then to her heart his piercing eyes fhot fire,
Which *Cupid* blows and rais'd into a flame,
That warms her zeal to invocate his name.
No part of *Jones* but in her eye exceeds
All humane fhape; fome god he muft be needs.
But when at her requeft he doth relate
The chances of his paft and prefent ftate;
Never was ear with *Orpheus* harp poffeft
As hers with *Jones*, whil'ft he his life expreft.

Thofe

These that have warm'd themselves by these strong
(fires
May eas'ly guess what fruits her wild desires
Produc'd to *Jones* ; The observance of the Court,
With feasts and banquets, and all Princely sport,
Are at his foot : he cannot name nor wish
That meat he likes, but straight 'tis in his dish.
In this high state some months he takes his ease,
Whil'st this sick Princess feeds on her disease :
At last a sharp alarm damps these desires,
Which threatned death, but could not quench her fires.
A Prince there was, mighty in bulk and mind,
Whose Kingdoms confines unto *No land* joyn'd :
Descended in his race from *Og* of *Basan* ;
You'd think his very name might well amaze one ,
Bahader Cham Mombaza's King ; h'had been
A long hot suiter to this mighty Queen,
But still repuls'd : now this unruly fire
Supprest with scorn, breaks forth from love to ire.
A mighty host he rais'd, and marcheth through
The heart of *No-land*, to command, not wooe :
Approaching neer her Court, he sends her word
She must be his own Queen at bed and board,
Or see her Kingdom burn in higher flames,
Then his for her : yet (for his spirit shames
To war with women) if she can find out
One man in all her Realm, that is so stout,
In her defence, with him his sword to try,
He'l bravely win her, or he'l bravely dye.
Her Courtiers quail'd at this, who knew his force

                                              Coul

ould not be parallel'd by man nor horse.
Nor could it choose but make the Queen look black,
Not pale. Th'Interpreter at *Jones* his back
Sounds in his ear this proud imperious speech ;
Had she been thence, h'had bid him kiss his breech
For this proud message : up howere he starts,
And this loud answer with his mouth he farts ;
So tell *Bahader Cham, Mombaza's* King,
One *Mars* begot in's wrath will have a fling
With him ere night; that one who at one breath
Don Dego and *Gonzago* did to death,
Will look him dead ; nor will I only be
This Princess champion, but (thy *Cham* to see)
He walk through beds of Scorpions : for I hear
He dares enough, and I can brook no peer.
This high reply nere mov'd the haughty *Cham*,
Let *Jones* be what he will, he's still the same.
The day's his own before the fights begun,
Were *Mars* himself instead of *Mars* his Son.
A back and brest and helmet strong he dond,
Well wrought and varnish'd by some Indian hand,
A whale-bone bow he takes of special strength,
With arrows barb'd, at least two yards in length :
A crooked Scimiter whose edge was flint,
Queintly conjoyn'd, and some tough spell was in't,
To make it proof against the strength of steel.
Oft had this sword made head-strong Giants reel.
By his right side a massie Mace he hangs,
With which his sturdy foes to death he bangs.
A buckler like a Spanish ruff he wore

About

About his neck, full half yard deep, or more :
He wore not this for his defence, or grace,
But to keep off his urine from his face.
For you mult know that member was still mounted :
The bravest womans man on earth accounted.
And thus prepar'd, this lusty Termagent,
Ascends his Castle on his Elephant.
And then advanceth to a spacious Green,
Before the Castle of this maiden Queen.
A brave *Arabian* courfer is prepar'd
For *Jones*, his own true arms he dons for guard,
Llewellins sword to do ; and so descends
Down to the Green, where the fierce *Cham* attends.
Jones was to seek what kind of fight were best,
To make against this Gyant and his beast.
Both far exceed in strength himself and horse,
And therefore art now must be joyn'd with force :
No breft to breft, a nimble charge, and gone,
His ready steed as foon comes off as on.
Had not the well-try'd arms he wore prov'd true,
The *Chams* smart whale-bone bow had made him rue
This bold attempt : but what can whales weak bones,
When whales themfelves come short to swallow
                                        (Jones
Thus thrice he charg'd, and thrice he came off clear,
At last he came close up in full career,
And turning short, the horses hind feet slipt :
Through which mischance the Carry-castle ript
His bowels forth with's tusk ; down falls the horse :
The furious beast clasps *Jones* with his proboscie ;

                                            And

nd mounts him high : but in his rife he found
he means to give *Behaders* face a wound;
nd cuts, in th'inftant, off the trunk that clafpt him :
o down the Elephant was forc'r to caft him.
his hard exploit none ere perform'd before,
ut one cf *Cafars* Soldiers, and no more.
he wounded beaft inrag'd with pain cries *Read the Commenta-ries de bello Africano.*
              (out
Vith hideous voice , and plung'd and
            (branc'd about
he Green, till from his feat the Prince he throw'th,
nd then (for by the *Cham*, from his firft growth,
his feat he had been taught) though mad with pain,
le ftrives to mount him on his back again.
ut *Jones* had lopt off his ftrong trunk before,
hereby he could perform this feat no more.
ere *Jones* denies he bred this docile beaft,
aught to his hand, he got him in the Eaft ; * *Read Curtius, touching that Ele-phant of Porus, who often re-mounted his mafter with his trunk in that battel between him and Alexander.*
nd his report muft have belief before us,
ho fwears it was the fame that carry'd
            (* *Porus*
gainft the *Macedon.* I cannot fee   (be,
w by wife natures rules this thing fhould
lefs in *Pliny's* Volumes it appears,
at Elephants may live two thoufand years.
w *Jones* leaps up in hafte, and fwiftly flyes,
th fword in hand, where bruis'd *Behader*
            (lyes ;
d ere he could get up, one fwafhing ftroke
head & buckler from his fhoulders took ;

Which

Which when 'twas off, they may compare't that will,
To the grim St. *Johns* head on *Ludgate-hill.*
His numerous army struck with grief and fright
At his sad fate, betook it self to flight.
And thus was *No-lands* Queen redeem'd by *Jones*
From bondage, rape, and *No-lands* loss at once,
Now, if she lov'd our Captain well before,
In reason she must love him ten times more,
Which she exprest by laying at his foot
Her people, *No-land*, and her self to boot :
But, whether 'twas the god of loves deep curse,
That she refus'd, for better or for worse,
Those mighty Princes which to her he sent,
To make her dote on a non-resident ;
Flings snow-balls at his heart, and flames at hers;
To keep conjunction from these errant Stars;
Or whether *Jones* his genitals had got
Some lame defect by *Skinks* late desperate shot.
And so his noble heart made him refuse
What having got he could not rightly use.
'Tis not in me to judge; but this I know,
Her violent fires scorcht her, and him his snow
So coold, that to avoid her amorous sight
He leaves her Court, and steals to sea by night.
So *Jason* us'd *Medea* erst, but hee's
So wise to take with him the golden fleece,
Which *Jones* contemn'd to do, and thought himself,
When safe return'd, his countries Mine of wealth.
No certain ground I have here to relate
This great deserted Queens unhappy fate :

B

But Sir *John Mandevils*, who doth deliver,
As *Jones* reports, he came soon after thither,
And found the peoples out-side all in black;
A sad expression for their Princes wrack.
Who told him, lately there arriv'd a man,
All white, who for them wondrous things had done:
Redeem'd their Queen and Kingdom from the shame
Of rape and rapine, which *Bahader Cham*
Came there to act, and was in open field,
By this white man, in single combate kill'd.
Their Queen enamor'd with this matchless man,
Refus'd and left by him: when nothing can
Quench her wild fires but Carthage Queens hard fate,
Whilst on the Cliff with pensive thoughts she sate,
A sudden spring she gave, and so commends
Her self to sea, where life and love she ends.
No more of this sad stuff: let's all at once
Joyn in a joyful welcome home to *Jones.*
In six months sail he steers by *Godwin* sands,
Casts Anchor at the Downs: the next day lands,
Hastes to the Queen at *London*, there express s
Every particular of his addresses
To *Prester John*; the great affairs success
As she desir'd: Lastly, in his progress,
He might have married the great Queen of *No-land*,
But this the Queen gave credit to at no hand,
Till 'twas confirm'd by Sir *John Mandevil*,
Whose strange reports they may believe that will.
Now let us well observe the happy Fate,
Which still provided for the Queen and State.

G

Jones

Jones had not rested fully three dayes here,
But out there breaks a great and fearful fire
Of strong rebellion ; and to quench it, none's
So fit, in common sence, as Captain *Jones.*
Brave *Essex* through affronts turn'd male-content,
Hatches in 's breast a desperate intent,
To seize the Person of the Queen, and those
He found most near about her, his strong foes.
Her Grace and Council call for *Jones*, to know
What in his judgment now were best to do.
Who first her gracious pardon doth beseech,
And then delivers this short pithy speech.
First guard the Court with *Westminsters* strong bands
Call in the neighbouring Counties by commands.
Out with your houshold men, shut up your Gates ;
We'l make your foes turn tail with broken pates.
Then call to you the richest of your Citts,
But seek no cash ; for in their bags their wits
Are close knit up : but onely thus much make
Them know, their wives and fortunes lye at stake ;
That they shall want no succour, whilst your hand
Can grasp the sword, and Scepter of this Land.
Thus arm their hearts, & rouze them from their beds
And then let us alone to arm their heads.
She now requires, that *Jones* in person go
To *Essex*, his intents to sound and know ;
To use all fairest means that may reduce him
From those leud wayes to which lost men seduce him
He undertakes it ; hastens to the Lord,
And is admitted in as soon as heard.

An

And here he finds Sr. *Walter Rawleigh* with him ;
some ill was in't, his fancy straight doth give him.
He knew he came not to the Earl for good,
But to provoke him to some madder mood.
Therefore from thence our *Jones* doth *Rawleigh* rate,
Shaking his martial truncheon o're his pate :
Bids him pack thence to th' knaves of his Grand Jury,
He'l make him else th'example of his fury.
Rawleigh was wife, and rul'd by his best sense,
Gives place to time, and so withdraws from thence.
Then *Jones* these Counsels to the Earl began,
How full of dangers were the wayes he ran.
How weak his power ; much less unto the force
Of *Englands*, than his Rain-deer's to a horse.
Thus his brave Family must be destroy'd,
His honours lost, his ancient house made void :
Besides, his cause was naught ; for though himself
Were read the Laws of this great Common-wealth,
Yet he had heard some Lawyer say long since,
There was no law to captivate our Prince.
Thus all the harmless blood that shall be spilt
In this bad cause, must lye on *Essex* guilt.
Lay hand on heart, most noble peer, (quoth *Jones*)
The Queen can pardon, and enrich at once.
Be you but good, she can be gracious,
Your own experience can inform you thus.
Thus *Jones* possest his noble heart so far,
He is resolv'd to wave the chance of war ;
Himself and house he yields unto the Queen,
And her cold mercy, which too soon was seen.

This

This is the laſt great act I can relate,
Of his good ſervice for the Queen and State:
Rewards fit for his worth there were prepar'd,
Which his high ſpirit paſt by without regard:
And his great Queen was ſeriouſly bent
To put him in ſome place of government;
But nature onely taught the man to fight,
And his rude Mother not to read and write.
Which was the chiefeſt cauſe that made him hate
To be imploy'd in myſteries of State.
Beſides, he was not pleaſed that her Grace
Cut off this Noble man before his face,
Whom he brought in; it may be his own lot,
With ax or cord for nought to go to pot.
Thus ignorance, a diſcontented mind,
And worth ill weigh'd, do make him fall behind
Occaſions lock; which loſt he never more,
Though bred and breath'd on hills, ſhall get before.
Now time and bruiſes, and much loſs of blood,
Had made Jones feel cold age was not ſo good
A fiery youth; he needs muſt find a fail
Of what he was; declin'd from top to tail.
Which made him wiſh he might put up his reſt,
And breathe his laſt in his own Countries breſt.
And for this cauſe he went unto her Grace,
And begg'd of her a Muſter-maſters place,
In *Wales*, near his firſt home: where he may ſpend
His later dayes in peace, and in it end:
And yet to leave behind his martial art,
To *Wale's* poſterity, before he part.

Thi

his fute with fpeed and readinefs is granted,
.nd fo to *Wales* our Mufter-mafter's janted.
Iere many years he fpent in telling more,
)r lefs, of thofe ftrange things he did before :
.t laft, in his old age, he grows fo wild,
Ie needs muft marry, to beget a child.
Vhich though he mift, the maftery he muft have
)'re every fex, *Jones* fent her to her grave.
)evotion now with his old age increaft,
Ie meditates thrice every day at leaft.
Iis only prayer was the Abfolution,
n our old Liturgy, with fome confufion
)f fhort ejaculations in his bed,
'or fome old flips, and for the blood he fhed ;
Efpecially for thofe fix Kings he kill'd,
Vithout remorfe, at the Juzippian field :
Ar laft death comes, whofe power he defi'd
'rom firft to laft ; and, thus he liv'd and di'd.
   Now, you wild blades that make loofe Inns your ftage
To vapour forth the acts of this fad age,
Your *Edghill* fight, the *Newberies* and the Weft,
And Northern clafhes ; where you ftill fought beft :
Your ftrange efcapes, your dangers voyd of fear,
When bullets flew between the head and ear :
Your *pia maters* rent, perifht your guts,
Yet live, as then ye had been but earthen buts :
Whether you fought by Dam me, or the Spirit,
To you I fpeak, ftill waving men of merit,
Be modeft in your tales, if you exceed
My Captain's hard achievements, I'le proceed

Once

Once more to imp my rural muses wings,
And tune my lyre so high, I'le break her strings,
But I will reach ye, and thence raise such laughter,
As shall continue for five ages after.

The Captains Elegie.

ANd art thou gone brave man? hath conquering death
  Put a full period to thy blustering breath?
Thus hath she plaid her master-piece? and here
Fixt her nil supra on thy sable biere?
Scap'st thou those hideous storms, those horrid fights
With many Giants, cruel beasts, fierce Knights?
Such dangerous stratagems, such foes intrapping,
And now hath death don't? sure he took thee napping;
For hadst thou been awake to use thy sword,
She would have shun'd thee, and have ta'ne thy word
For thy appearance, till the last return
Of her long term. Or did thy mettle burn
Through thy chapt clay unto Elysiums shades
T'incounter with the ghosts of those old blades,
Great Cæsar, Scipio, Hannibal; 'cause here
Thy fiery spirit could not find its peer?
How couldst thou else find time to fold thy arms
In thy still grave, now Mars rains bloody storms
On Christian earth? great Austria would be ours
Without pitcht field, without beleaguering towers:
Wert thou but here, thy swo d would strike the stroke
To break or bring their necks to Britains yoke.

Per

erhaps it was the providence of *Fate*,
o snatch thee up, lest thou should'st come too late,
low souldiers drop pel-mel, whose souls might thrust
hine from the chiefest place, which thou from first
last gain'd on earth ; now what shall England do ?
imp like some grandame that hath lost her shooe.
ut case a new Tyrone again should spring
rom his old urn, or some such furious thing
ls fierce Mac-kil-cow, where were then our Jones,
o bring these Rebels on their marrow bones ?
Dr say, gainst Spain our pikes we re-advance,
or their old Sack, as such a thing may chance,
where shall we then find out that Martial man,
hat kill'd six thousand with nine score ? he's gone.
Aud we that lick the dish that Homer lapt in,
What fury now shall our dull brains be rapt in ?
Ve must go sing Sr. Lancelot, and rehearse
Dld Huan's villanous prose in wilder verse ;
Or else put up our pipes, and all at once,
ry, farewell wit : all's gone with Captain Jones.
Vell, go thy wayes (old blade th'hast done thy share
or things beyond belief ; time (never fear)
Vill give thee being here : th'hast left us stuff
To build thy Pyramid, more than enough,
To equal Cayre's, and haply 'twil out-last it,
So with thy glorious deeds we may rough cast it.
arewel great soul, and take this praise with many,
Except thy foes, thou nere didst harm to any :
And thus far let our Muse thy loss deplore,
Vell she may sigh, but she shall nere sing more.

His

His Epitaph.

Tread softly (mortals) ore the bones
   Of the worlds wonder, Captain Jones?
who told his glorious deeds to many,
But never was believ'd of any :
Posterity, let this suffice,
He swore all's true, yet here he lyes.

FINIS.

www.ingramcontent.com/pod-product-compliance
Lightning Source LLC
Chambersburg PA
CBHW032205010726
47493CB00008BA/2831